HORDE'S POWER

Starbarian Saga Book Two

ROBERT JESCHONEK

STARBARIAN SAGA BOOK TWO:
HORDE'S POWER

Published by Blastoff Books
411 Chancellor Street
Johnstown, Pennsylvania 15904

PART I
WELCOME TO THE JUNGLE

CHAPTER 1

JUNGLEWORLD, 3 weeks after the Battle of Io

LIGHTNING BLAZED NEARBY, FLARING THROUGH THE downpour of rain. It briefly lit the figure of a heavily muscled man with long blond hair crouching in the shadows of the emerald jungle.

As booming thunder followed the lightning, he watched his target—a beast that looked like a cross between a dark blue gorilla, a ram, and a porcupine, stalking through the dense brush. It stopped suddenly and raised its head, listening, its bright blue bulbous ears twitching.

The man with the long blond hair froze, but not out of fear. Fear was an emotion that never drove a barbarian Horde Lord under any circumstances, no matter the odds against him.

And he, Tork Gallgore, was just such a Horde Lord.

The beast snorted, shook its head roughly, and resumed stalking. It looked for all the world like a wild predator on the hunt, following only the evidence of its senses in pursuit through the trackless jungle.

The evidence of its senses and the boxy, palm-sized device with the glowing blue screen and gold buttons gripped in its clawed tentacle.

How many like that beast—a thing called a Narl—had Tork killed in the weeks he'd been on the jungle planet? How many scars did he bear on his body from the spines and claws and acid venom they wielded?

Yet the Narl kept on coming, always patrolling, always hunting. And if there had been some doubt, when Tork first arrived, about their role in the scheme of things on this planet, it was long gone.

It had died the first time Tork had seen one slaughter and devour one of the local villagers.

Again, lightning flared from above, illuminating the jungle. Tork squinted in the flash of bright light, trying to keep his eyes locked on the enemy...and quickly realized the Narl was gone. The huge blue creature had disappeared.

Heart pounding as thunder boomed, Tork flicked his head from side to side without catching sight of the missing Narl. He breathed deep, seeking the beast's characteristic rank scent...and found no luck that way, either.

He might have thought the Narl had simply vanished if not for the clenching of his gut. That feeling told him, as it had thousands of times before, that the danger had not passed, and his target was still close.

Cautiously, Tork took a step forward. He adjusted his

grip on the curved handle of his battleaxe, keeping his fingers wrapped around it as tightly as he dared. The round, crimson gem between the blade and the spike was dark, waiting for him to push the button and fill it with power.

He took another step, all his senses fully engaged. Had they ever been so attuned back on desolate planet Earth before he'd come to this jungle world? He didn't think so.

Perhaps passing through the portal from Io weeks ago had changed him. Or maybe it was just that he hadn't stopped fighting to survive since arriving here.

Whatever the reason, he felt at one with the fierce new world...which was why the Narl shouldn't have been able to surprise him the way it did.

Roaring, the beast dropped down out of a tree, crashing onto him like a ton of solid rock.

As Tork buckled under the impact, the Narl's spines dug into the flesh of his shoulders and back, punching deep. Its ram horns bashed into the back of his head, and its tentacles wrapped around his chest, their thorny ridges sinking into his pectoral meat.

Tork realized he had scant seconds to turn the tables. As the creature's hot breath blasted his neck, he knew a jet of acid venom would not be far behind.

Thumbing the button on the handle of the battleaxe, Tork felt the weapon hum to life in his hands. With a roar of his own, he swung it up and back, punching the spike on its heel into the body of the beast on his shoulders.

The Narl howled in pain as the spike plunged into it, crackling with electrical force. Tork tugged on the handle, raking the charged spike through the creature's flesh and bone like a hot blade through butter.

As soon as the Narl fell away, Tork yanked the spike free and whirled, sweeping the weapon up over his head. The beast rolled over fast and wrenched its mouth open in a familiar, deadly pose.

But Tork didn't give it time to spew a jet of sizzling acid at him. Heaving the axe down hard, he cleaved the Narl's skull in half from forehead to chin. Both sides splashed into the mud, bubbling with the reservoir of acid that had been nearly ejected in Tork's direction.

As Tork wrenched the axe from the skull of the dead beast, electrical bolts crackled along its blade and spike, small scale twins of the lightning that again burst from the sky. Any acid that had touched the miraculous metal was neutralized and burned away, leaving the weapon pristine and ready to kill again.

Ready, in other words, to keep Tork alive another day, another hour, another minute in this most hostile environment…always in the hope that he might yet find a way home.

Though with every day that passed, that hope became a little fainter. His sacrifice, single-handedly slamming shut the portal between Io and Jungleworld to keep the Caul from moving closer to Earth, was looking more and more like a one-way trip.

Suddenly, another boom of thunder crashed through the jungle…and then, after a moment, another. Tork scowled; if the second boom was thunder, too, there should have been lightning first.

Gazing up into the curtain of rain, he quickly spotted

the cause of the noise—a sleek silver fighter drone racing overhead. As he watched its progress through gaps in the canopy, the fighter zoomed past at a high rate of speed, on its way to a battle or another pressing mission.

That was one of the first things Tork had learned on that hostile planet. For the killers and fighters of the Caul, there was always another pressing mission to race off to.

Thumbing off power to the battleaxe, he backed away from the dead Narl, preparing to melt away into the foliage. It was something he had a real talent for, considering he'd never lived in a jungle before. In the desolate landscape of Earth, at least the part of it where he'd spent his life, he'd never even seen an actual jungle.

Before Tork could slip away, however, the fighter's engine screamed, and it whipped around to swoop back toward him. The red light of a detection beam flared to life on its belly, stabbing into the canopy not far from his position.

As the light slid toward him, he spun and charged into the brush. Though he had brought down his share of drones, their guns could still kill him on the spot if he took an unlucky step and ended up in the crosshairs. He'd seen too many others blown to bits by those guns to take them lightly.

Just as he jumped a rushing stream, though, the broad green tail of a water beast lurking under the surface lashed up and swatted his left leg hard enough to knock him off balance. He toppled on the muddy opposite bank, rolling through the impact but grounded for the moment.

Meanwhile, the red detection beam sliced through the grove, following the path he'd taken. His heart beat faster as it swiftly cruised toward him; if it tagged him, the drone's guns would open fire without hesitation.

Tork scrambled in the muck, eager to bolt deeper into the jungle. He got one foot under him, then the other, as the red beam cut ever closer, its brightness intensifying as it approached.

He slipped again, though, and dropped to one knee. Using his battleaxe for support, he regained his footing, but he didn't know if he could evade the beam in time to escape the impending gunfire.

Suddenly, then, a shimmering figure came to life in front of him. It was more like the outline of a humanoid creature than an actual lifeform—a rippling shape whose skin swirled with rainbow colors and a silvery sheen like a slick of oil on water.

The shape was as tall and broad as Tork but feature-less. Its intentions were unreadable—at least if you hadn't encountered its kind before.

The shape wavered, its indistinct edges surrounded by a soft white halo. Its sides flexed, armlike appendages separating from the central mass and reaching toward Tork.

Sensing the red beam approaching from behind him, Tork did not resist the touch of the shimmering thing. His skin tingled as it took hold of his muscular forearms, the silvery, slick-like substance wrapping around them like liquid mercury.

Then, with a sudden snap, the thing wrenched him forward, hauling him through the outline of its form. As the red beam slid over the spot where he'd been standing a heartbeat ago, he disappeared, entering the flattened shape without emerging on the other side.

The shimmering thing followed, sucking inward, draining into a single point in midair which then winked out before the red light sliced through and continued along its way.

CHAPTER 2

ABOARD THE BATTLESHIP HELLCYON, somewhere between Earth and Mars

"DEMON SPAWN!" VIXA SNARLED AND SLASHED WITH THE obsidian dagger, her long black hair flying. "I'll chop you into salad!"

"How *dare* you?" The plant-man with a flower for a face stretched his green stalk of a body out of the path of the blade, then slung himself around to dodge the backslash. "Perhaps *I* should chop *you* into *hamburger!*"

Vixa spun and leaped, going for the throat—moving so fast she nicked it before the plant man sprang out of range again. Her supporters, the men and women of her horde, howled with delight, cheering her on.

"You think you can tell *us* to fight alongside the scum of the Eastern Horde?" Vixa laughed bitterly, scrawling the dagger through the air in front of her. "We would sooner *die!* Or better yet, *slaughter* every last one of them!"

The walking plant, whose name was Punji Imbroglio, rustled the indigo petals of his face flower, which were mottled with white flecks like stars in the darkness of space. "Wonderful idea, my brilliant friend! Do the Caul's work *for* them. Pure genius!"

"Shut *up!*" Vixa leaped, driving the knife at Punji...and he responded by blowing a cloud of glittering golden pollen all over her. Coughing and flailing, she fell in mid-leap, dropping the dagger as she fell toward the hard floor of the vast hangar deck.

At which point, Punji gracefully swept himself around, fanned out the vines of his midsection in a kind of net, and caught her before she hit.

"Let me go!" Vixa thrashed, trying to fling herself out of the net. "Put me down right *now!*"

"Only if you promise not to slaughter the Southern Horde!" snapped Punji. "That's in violation of the truce and you know it!"

"Slaughter *you* instead!" shouted Vixa.

"I'm not feeling the spirit of cooperation!" Punji twisted the net around her and squeezed. "Maybe a *group hug* will coax it out of hiding!"

Just then, a thunderous voice boomed through the cavernous chamber. "*Release her!*"

Punji didn't hesitate to unwind the fibrous net from his captive. Vixa rolled out, snatched the dagger from the floor, and spun, ready to plunge it into the plant-man's face.

But she froze when the booming voice called out again. "*Vixa, stop!*"

She did as she was told, then slowly turned toward the voice.

Angar Crux, her barbarian husband, stormed up with broadsword in hand, his face etched with fury.

"What is this about?" he snarled. "What is happening here?"

Vixa lunged toward him. "*Someone* has to stand up for our people!" She jabbed the point of the dagger in Punji's direction. "*This* one wants to put us at the mercy of the damned *Eastern Horde.*"

"No! Never!" Angar swung his broadsword in a fast figure eight.

"He said our hordes must *merge* and train together for *battle!*" said Vixa. "He said we must trust the *Easterners* with our very *lives!*"

"This can't be!" snapped Angar.

"Look at them!" Vixa swept the dagger toward the crowd of humans gathered along the far wall. "*Animals!* As if *they* could ever be *trusted!*"

"Unbelievable!" Angar pointed his sword at Punji. "Who *gave* this order, you wicked weed? Who *told* you to mix our hordes together for the purpose of fighting a *war?*"

"*You* did, Horde Lord." Punji bobbed his flower of a face the way he did when he was laughing. "*You* were the one who gave the order."

Angar sneered at Vixa. "And *you* are expected to *follow* it, my wife!"

Vixa fumed, opening her mouth to say something.

But Angar cut her off. "You will *all* follow the order, as *I* am your Horde Lord! And *you*." He turned his gaze on the Easterners along the wall. "You will *also* obey me! Without Tork Gallgore here, I am *your* Horde Lord, too!"

The hangar was dead silent as he looked around at its occupants—the ranks of longtime enemies arrayed on either side. Then, swinging his broadsword overhead, he marched on them...Easterners first, then Southerners, herding them away from the walls.

Roaring, he drove the two hordes together like cattle. They ended up falling over each other in one big cluster in the middle of the room.

"Now!" Angar crashed his blade against the metal floor with an echoing clang. "You all have *one choice!* Join forces to save our *home* and all the *universe* from the greatest adversary of all *time!*"

Some of the people nodded and murmured in agreement.

"*He* is my *right hand* in all things!" Angar pointed the sword at Punji. "If you disobey or displease *him*, you offend *me!* And you will pay *dearly* for that offense."

This time, *all* of the people nodded.

"Now get to work! You must *prepare* for the *ultimate* war!" With that, Angar spun on his heel and stomped across the hangar, turning just once on his way out the door to cast a final baleful glare upon the mixed mob of barbarians who were now *all* his subjects.

At least until he brought their Horde Lord back from beyond the pale.

But *could* he? Somehow, Angar knew Tork was still alive; he felt his presence, far away, like a bright, beckoning star. But bringing him home, he knew, might be impossible.

According to the Blacksmiths—wielders of the miraculous science that had created the *Hellcyon*—it would be a challenge unlike any other. Based on their analysis of Angar's link to Tork and the remnants of the Io portal, they had found his probable location...but it was distant and deep inside Caul territory. The Blacksmiths didn't think they were ready to go so far behind enemy lines and conquer Caul forces just yet.

But maybe by the time they got there, they'd be seasoned enough. Maybe, with training from the savage peoples of the Easter and Southern hordes, their killer instincts would be fully awakened.

Or Angar and the hordes would learn enough about science and the ship to take over and fight the war alone. That was what he was planning to do, after all, sooner or later. The Blacksmiths were fools if they didn't expect it.

It was really just a matter of when exactly he decided to make his move.

CHAPTER 3

JUNGLEWORLD

"SHANG!" THAT CURSE WAS THE FIRST WORD OUT OF TORK'S mouth when he fell from the shimmering being and hit the rocky floor of the cave.

He came down hard, taking most of the impact on his beefy shoulders and hitting his head along the way on a lump of rock. He never let go of his battleaxe, though, and popped up into a crouch with it brandished before him.

"Who are you?" He blinked hard at the silver film on his eyes and face, wiped them on his hairy bicep. "Where am I?"

The humanoid shape just stood there, its surface rippling with rainbow hues bathed in a silvery sheen. Now that Tork was away from the surface noise of rain, thunder, and the pursuing airborne drone, he could hear it made a soft sound like the buzzing of a bumblebee as it swayed.

"How did you bring me here?" asked Tork. "And why?"

Finally, the being spoke, its voice like a whispering wind. *"Help. Need help."*

"I am a Horde Lord!" snapped Tork. "I *never* need help!"

"Not you," said the shimmering thing. *"We. We need you help us."*

Tork narrowed his eyes. "You need my help how?"

"Destroy invaders." The being wavered out of focus, then back in again, its silver sheen becoming ruby red. *"Make stop. Make die."*

"I've been doing that since I got here," said Tork. "I've been doing the best I can."

"Not enough," said the being. *"No time."*

Slowly, Tork lowered the axe. "No time for what?"

"Destroy all now, or no everything all."

Tork frowned. "Know everything?"

"No everything all."

"I don't understand." Tork shook his head. "You're not making sense."

"Wait." With a hissing sound, the being sucked into itself, its shimmering substance yanking in from all edges into a central point like a navel. Seconds later, another form burst out of the navel, quickly stretching into a new shape that took the place of the ethereal slick.

Unlike the original shape, the new one was dense and compact, perfectly solid. It had sharp, square edges and a gleaming black surface like obsidian stone.

It made a noise like gravel scraping together and spoke, gazing up at Tork from knee level with blazing red eyes. "No more everything." The new creature's voice was rough and deep, its words clear as the cracking of rock by a chisel. "That is what we were trying to tell you."

"You mean the invaders will destroy your world?" said Tork.

The creature spread its four stubby arms as wide as they would go. "They will destroy everything."

"I am a Horde Lord, but I am only one man. I've been fighting for weeks, and I've barely put a dent in their forces."

"Because you weren't working with *us*."

Tork shook his head. "You haven't done much on your own that I've seen."

"We did at first," said the creature. "Until they started singing to us."

"Singing?" Tork scowled.

"Sending their Song around the world. Filling our heads with it every minute of every day. Twisting what we can do."

"Some kind of dark magic, you mean," said Tork. "Or science."

"We don't understand how it works," said the creature. "But we know where it comes from. We know the place."

"And you haven't stopped it?"

"We can't get close enough, and we couldn't stop it if we did. We need help. Someone to destroy the Song and set us free. Someone like *you*."

Tork was silent for a moment, considering what he'd heard. His main goal, the reason he'd been fighting so hard, was just to survive and get back to the *Hellcyon*. But what if the creature and his people could help make all that happen?

Maybe, by fighting a war for someone he didn't know, Tork could get exactly what he wanted.

"Who exactly are you people, anyway?" he asked. "What do you call yourselves?"

"We call ourselves the Gossa." The creature touched its head with all four of its three-fingered hands. "And *I* am called Rogg."

"All right, Rogg." Tork permitted a slight smile to cross his bearded face. "I will do what I can for your people. I will spill *much* blood and lay waste to all that troubles us."

"Thank you." Rogg's eyes flashed with ruby light. "Finally, we Gossa have hope. We have a path to regain this world as our own...all because of you, our angel of death and vengeance."

"When do we start on this path?" asked Tork. "When does our mission begin?"

"Why not now?" Again, Rogg's eyes flashed like red beacons. "Why not this very moment, my friend?"

CHAPTER 4

HELLCYON

AS USUAL, ANGAR WAS THE LAST ONE TO WALK INTO THE conference room. Everyone else who'd been invited to the meeting was already seated around the big, elliptical table.

Also as usual, no one said anything about it. Either they were too afraid to call him on it, or they just knew it would do no good.

In his months aboard the *Hellcyon,* Angar had taught them well.

With a nod, he took his usual seat at the end of the table closest to the door. The plastic chair creaked under his weight, like always, and he leaned back in it.

"All right everybody." Finn Gauge, the captain of the ship and leader of the Blacksmiths, got to his feet at the far end of the table. He looked frazzled—his brown and gray hair mussed, his bright blue eyes bloodshot, his expression grim. "Time to make the call. Should we start the countdown?"

"Good question." Chief Scientist Isabel Haussmann folded her arms on the table and leaned forward. "I don't suppose we'd consider waiting till we're ready?"

Gauge sighed. "Admittedly, our current posture is not optimal."

"Understatements, anyone?" Punji, the *Hellcyon's* Tactical Chief, shook his indigo face-petals for emphasis.

"Agreed." The crystalline form of Major Lavish Schist, head of security, turned icy pink with annoyance. "Our readiness is *sorely* lacking."

"Then what do you recommend?" Gauge wasn't happy, either. "Go back to Earth and wait for the Caul to come to us?"

"Not to mention, give up on Tork Gallgore?" Valla Viss, the half-spider/half-snake leader of the *Hellcyon's* fighter squadrons, wagged her hairy spider head. "Let him rot out there in the depthssss of Caul sssspaccce?"

Angar eyed her, impressed by her continued devotion. As Tork's second-in-command at the Battle of Io, she'd been the last to see him before his leap through the portal.

"Here's a scenario to consider," said Isabel. "What if we move against the Caul before we're completely ready, and they wipe us out? They obliterate the *Hellcyon.*" Her green-eyed gaze was piercing as it fixed on Gauge. "What then? All our work for nothing. The last hope of the galaxy—maybe even the universe—gone forever."

"Not the first time that scenario has occurred to me." The tendons in Gauge's neck stood out as he flattened his hands on the table. "But it's not our only consideration.

Unless we recover Tork, our odds of ultimate success are dramatically reduced. You know this."

"And we're *sure* we haven't already lost him for good?" said Isabel.

Angar cleared his throat loudly then. "Tork lives," he said simply.

All eyes turned to him. On two subjects, he was the acknowledged expert aboard the ship—the killer instinct and the status of Tork Gallgore.

The two were bound together somehow, in ways far deeper and stronger than the Blowback link devised by the Blacksmiths to keep them from killing each other. Ironically, the two arch-enemies were connected, even across the vast gulf of space. Angar now had the capability of saving the life of the man he'd dreamed of slaughtering for most of his adult life.

And he was determined to save his enemy at almost any cost.

"You need him, don't you?" Angar looked around the table coolly, meeting each gaze in turn. "You just said, having both of us is your best chance of defeating the Caul."

Gauge nodded slowly. "Correct."

"Then it seems to me we should begin the countdown." Angar got up from his chair. "We should get Tork back before he dies."

"Issss he in *danger* of dying?" Valla sounded worried.

"Oh yes," said Angar. "That much comes through the link clearly. He has been in terrible danger since the moment he went through the portal."

"From what?" asked Valla.

Angar shrugged. "I only get feelings, not details. Even his location is just a feeling, a sense of where he is. But if the feelings ever stop..." He banged the tip of his broadsword on the metal floor. "We should start the countdown and make our move before that happens. Especially if the galaxy—and the universe?—depend on the two of us together."

"Wow." Punji bobbed his flowery head, dusting the table with golden pollen. "Listen to you! Pushing to rescue the hated enemy you used to want to murder!"

Angar smirked. "Who says I don't still want to murder him?"

Punji laughed. "Spoken like a true barbarian!"

"*Former* barbarian," said Angar. "You people have civilized me, after all."

"Have we?" Isabel watched him with hooded eyes. "How do even know you're telling the truth about Tork's location?"

"What possible reason could he have for *not* telling the truth?" asked Schist.

"That's a good question." Isabel stayed focused on Angar. "I wonder if he has an answer for us."

Angar met her gaze, unflinching. Since the Battle of Io, he'd won over much of the crew—but Isabel kept her distance. Why, he didn't know.

Unless, maybe, she was picking up on what he was keeping hidden from everyone but himself.

Smirking, he waved her off and headed for the door. "Start the countdown," he said over his shoulder. "Risk everything while you still can."

As the door dissolved before him, he heard Punji

squawk from his spot at the table. "You heard the man! Let's do this thing!"

Then, as Angar walked out, he heard the final word direct from Gauge—the order from the captain of the ship.

The captain who was really just repeating what the barbarian had said a moment earlier.

"The word is given." He was speaking into the intercom, talking to someone in the ship's nerve center, the Cortex. "Start the countdown in 5 minutes at T-minus 12 hours."

"Yes sir," said a male voice over the speaker. "T-minus 12 hours, roger."

"It's set," said Gauge. "God help us all."

That was the last thing Angar heard from the conference room before the door reassembled behind him. He nodded with satisfaction as he continued down the hallway, happy that the meeting had gone his way.

Now if he could just make it to the woman he loved before one of his wives got in his way first.

CHAPTER 5

JUNGLEWORLD

BY THE TIME TORK AND ROGG EMERGED FROM underground, it was nearly nightfall. The jungle was well-drenched, with every leaf dripping, and the red sun was nearly all the way below the horizon.

The air was cool, as it so rarely was on Jungleworld, and smelled of wetness and plant life. The night beasts were crying out in all directions, welcoming the coming cover of darkness.

Tork breathed deep and smiled to himself as he followed his obsidian companion. He loved the jungle when it was like that, without the oppressive heat and blazing sun. The Caul patrols were less active, and the fierce daytime wildlife was absent. The ordeal of fighting for his life and being lost so far from home faded into the background, giving him time to collect his thoughts and appreciate the strange beauty of the world around him.

Though he knew, of course, it was destined not to last. Sooner or later, something would snap him back to the harsh reality that his life had become.

"Is it true that you eat your victims?" Rogg asked as he led Tork through the thick foliage. His gravelly voice was loud for someone who only came up to the level of Tork's knees. "I've heard that everyone you catch, you butcher, cook, and kill on the spot."

"Only if they've got enough meat on their bones." Tork kept his battleaxe drawn in case he needed it. After the weeks he'd spent on Jungleworld, he knew a new horror could leap out at him at any time.

The axe also came in handy as he hacked low-hanging branches and vines out of his way. Rogg, as low to the ground as he was, didn't need to do much clearing as he marched along—but Tork often had to chop away brush to keep it from smacking and scratching him. Not to mention, some of those vines and branches were more animal than plant and capable of strangling or biting him if he wasn't careful.

"How do your victims taste?" asked Rogg. "The Narl, for example?"

"Pretty gamy, to be honest," said Tork. "I'd steer clear, if I were you."

"What about the Skindle and Cossitora?"

"Never heard of them," said Tork. "But, you know, I don't always stop to learn the names of what I'm killing."

"I like that," said Rogg. "Just the kind of style I was looking for."

"Good to know." Tork thumbed the power stud on the axe and swung the blade through the air above Rogg's head, slashing a tangle of vines from his path. One of the vines squealed as it fell away, purple ichor draining from its tubular form.

"So I've been wondering about something," said Tork. "How can we understand each other if we're from different worlds?"

"Are we?" Rogg looked back at him with his flashing ruby eyes. "You mean you're from a different world, like the Caul and their people?"

"Well yes, but…"

"*Are* you one of the Caul's people, then?" asked Rogg. "A rogue invader, fighting to stop the other invaders?"

"No," said Tork. "I am *not* of the Caul. And you haven't answered my question."

"Then why *are* you killing so many of them?" asked Rogg. "What's with the one-man war?"

"Find out for yourself," snapped Tork. "Read my mind! Isn't that how you learned to speak my language?"

"Just tell me why you're killing them," said Rogg. "I want to hear you say it."

Frustrated, Tork swung the axe a few more times than necessary to clear away a mass of slithering pink tendrils. Why wouldn't Rogg just admit to reading his mind? It wasn't a big deal to Tork after his own telepathic experience with the Blacksmiths' thinklink system.

Clearly, he had a long way to go to understand the motivations of the obsidian-skinned Gossa.

"I am killing everyone who tries to kill me first," Tork told him at last. "Or who is trying to kill someone else. If they are part of the Caul, which is truly evil, then it pleases me even more."

For a moment, Rogg said nothing. His black surfaced glistened in the last gray light of dusk, gleaming like a half-submerged stone in a stream.

"Getting dark," he said finally, and then his eyes shone brighter, casting twin beams of ruby-red light into the vegetation ahead. "I don't need to rest, but perhaps you do."

"We can set up camp soon." Tork hacked another mass of slitherers drooping toward him. "The hunting beasts can be relentless in the heart of the night."

"On the other hand," said Rogg, "it's a very long way to the Singing Place. The sooner we get there, the sooner my people will be released from their torment."

"How far away is it, exactly?" asked Tork.

"Days, at least. It depends."

"On what?"

"On how many invaders we need to kill to get there," said Rogg. "And how many jungle beasts try to kill us."

"All right." Tork sighed. "A little further, then."

"Perfect." Rogg waved all four hands in a gesture that may have signified delight. "I'm glad we're on this quest together, Tork Gallgore...even if you *are* a bit cannibalistic for my civilized tastes. No offense, of course."

Tork rolled his eyes and shook his head. "None taken."

CHAPTER 6

HELLCYON

THE PROW OF THE *HELLCYON* WAS A HORNED DEATH'S HEAD with glowing red eyes. Like the skull and crossbones on the Jolly Roger flags of ancient pirate ships, the death's head was meant to strike fear in all enemies who saw it coming. When the war started, the Blacksmiths hoped, the symbol of the death's head blazing through space, leaving death and destruction in its wake, would terrify the Caul and inspire its victims to rise up and fight back against their conquerors.

As the center of symbolic fear and power aboard the ship, it was Angar's favorite part of the *Hellcyon*—as much of a "happy place" as he was likely to find. He went there to think, to scheme, to get away from it all…and, on days like this, to meet someone he cared deeply about for some special time together.

She wasn't there when he arrived, so he gazed out through the blazing red eyes at the starry darkness of space and thought about what had brought him to that point. When the Blacksmiths had first picked him up on Earth, along with his sworn enemy Tork Gallgore, he hadn't imagined they would take him into space—hadn't even known what space really was. He and Tork were needed to restore the Blacksmith's killer instincts, they'd been told, and help fight a war against the powerful and inhuman Caul and their allies. The first battle of that war, back on Jupiter's moon, Io, had extracted a terrible price; Tork had disappeared through a portal while keeping a Caul fleet from passing through to strike an early blow. The *Hellcyon* had returned to Earth, then, and picked up the Eastern and Southern Hordes to serve as reinforcements. Now, it was up to Angar to get those barbarians oriented, forge them into a fighting force, and turn them to the task of training the Blacksmiths to use violence against their powerful enemies.

Thinking back, it amazed Angar that he'd come so far and changed so much in so short a time. Not only did he know about space and alien species, but he knew about science, as well. Not only did he think before acting more than he'd ever done before, but he felt like he'd gained wisdom and patience...qualities he'd never imagined would someday be his. Then there was the way he'd been working with the Hordespeople, getting them just civilized enough to teach their fighting techniques to the crew.

There was another change, too, one he kept to himself.

All seven of his wives were aboard the ship now...but the woman he most wanted to see and spend time with was none of them.

"Angar?" The chiming, singsong voice of Lieutenant Quinza Acquiesce rang out behind him in the Skull, instantly making his heart beat faster.

It beat faster still when he turned and saw her—pale, glowing skin swirling with color...delicate, fuzzy antennae curling from her temples...butterflies instead of hair draping her head and shoulders. Every move she made was graceful, and every sound she made was musical.

She said she was a goddess from a beautiful, dead world, and he believed her. He longed to worship her, to offer prayers and make sacrifices in her name. She was like no one else he'd ever known.

"Hello, Quinza."

"You are doing it again." She tipped her head to one side, her bright yellow eyes fixed on him.

"Doing what?"

"Smiling." She nodded. "I've noticed you do it quite often when we are together."

"I wonder why." His smile widened.

Quinza smiled, too, and the butterflies on her head fluttered their colorful wings. "I'm glad we can bring each other happiness," she said, "even on the verge of conflict and the brink of the unknown."

"Yes." Angar took a step toward her and stopped. As always, he felt the need to take her in his arms, to kiss her...ravish her. His blood ran hot with desire, the almost overpowering urge to possess her in every way. But he held back, as he had from the beginning.

She seemed so fragile, he feared he might break her. She was so perfect, he feared she might reject him.

"Are you ready for what comes next?" she asked. "Whatever it might be?"

"Yes." He said it firmly, though he had his doubts. "I'm ready to fight the Caul. I was *born* ready."

"That isn't the next I meant," said Quinza.

He frowned. "I'm ready to find and rescue Tork Gallgore, too. The link between us is strong and will lead me right to him."

"That isn't what I meant, either," said Quinza. "What about what *you*? The life that comes after for you? The happiness you seek?"

He gazed at her, straining to read her face. Was she talking about his love for her? The happiness that could grow stronger between them?

Perhaps it was time to bare his soul, to tell her in full of his deepest feelings. Now might be the best time, the *only* time to do it.

But what if he got it wrong? He was in a different world aboard the *Hellcyon*, one in which certain rules were still hidden from him. Even as he was called to make that world more like his own, to make its people more savage like his own, he wasn't sure what to do next…at least with Quinza.

"It does no good to think too much about what comes after," he said. "Especially when war is in the cards. As ready for battle as I am, what comes after may be only darkness."

"But fooling ourselves is all that keeps us going sometimes, isn't it? And what if our tomorrow *does* come, and we aren't ready because we never dared imagine it?"

"I want to imagine it," he said. "I want that more than anything."

"I understand." When she said it, butterflies fluttered from her head and sailed toward him. They circled his own head, then lighted on his shoulders, waiting for what was coming next.

In that moment, it seemed to him a cord stretched between him and Quinza. If he told her how he felt, it seemed, their future could be assured. If he didn't, he might end up dying without saying the words he wanted to say to his truest love.

So why did he hold back? Mighty warrior that he was, used to facing every challenge with courage and power, why did he hesitate to tell her what he wanted? He'd never had trouble expressing himself to his seven wives or army of concubines, had he?

Maybe it was just because none of them had ever made him feel the way *she* did. Until he'd met her, he'd never even known he *could* feel that way.

"Quinza..." He swallowed hard, straining to get the words out. "Quinza...I am a Horde Lord. Without Tork, I am the *only* lord of *all* the hordes." Turning, he gazed into space through one of the Skull's fiery red eyes. "My responsibility is to my people alone. It doesn't really matter what *I* think I want."

"You're wrong." She stepped up beside him, her shoulder resting against his arm. "It *always* matters...especially for someone like you. Someone who is *special*. Someone who may have divinity coursing through him."

Angar frowned. "Divinity?"

"The power of a god," she said. "Or very nearly so."

He shook his head. "I'm no god."

"I've seen you breathing without air," said Quinza. "Without a helmet, after the dome fell at Io station. That was something no *human* should have been able to do."

Angar felt her eyes upon him, but he didn't meet her gaze. He hadn't discussed Io with her since they'd left that moon's orbit, and he'd hoped perhaps she'd forgotten or would drop the subject...but he should have known better. The more he got to know Quinza, the more he realized she missed nothing.

"If you *are* a god, it can be a wonderful thing," she told him. "It can change you in ways you never imagined."

"Have you told anyone?" He'd asked her not to.

"Of course not," said Quinza. "But you can't expect this to just go away. Take it from me, it won't. And you shouldn't *want* it to. It's a *gift*, Angar."

"A gift?"

"And it might be the start of something even more wonderful." She took his hand in her own and turned to face him. "What else can you do that you couldn't do before?"

He frowned. "Nothing."

"But you haven't exactly been *trying*, have you?" she asked. "You haven't been pushing yourself to the limit and beyond."

He didn't answer. The warmth of her hand around his was intoxicating.

"Maybe you're a little afraid," she said softly. "Afraid to find out what other powers you might have. Because then you'll have a new question to answer, won't you?"

He thought for a moment. "Who did this to me, you mean?"

"There's another one. The most important question of all." Quinza stood on tiptoe and lowered her voice to a whisper. "What will you do with these powers?"

For once, the urge to kiss her was not the foremost thought in his mind. The question she'd posed was one he hadn't considered—yet now that she'd said it aloud, he could think of little else.

What if she was right, and some kind of divine power had been given to him? Would he be best served using it in plain sight to fight the Caul and bring back Tork? Would it be better to keep it in his back pocket for an emergency, when nothing else could help him? Or would the best idea of all be to save it for the day he'd been planning from the start, from the first minute when he'd set foot aboard the *Hellcyon?* It would certainly make it easier to attain the definitive victory he craved.

Or maybe the answer to the question was something he hadn't thought of yet, something he might never conceive of on his own.

"What would *you* do?" he asked Quinza.

"You're asking the wrong question." Smiling, she gave his hand a squeeze. "It's not what *would* I do…it's what *do* I do every day of my life."

"Right." Angar had almost forgotten she'd been a goddess—and still was, though her worshippers were all gone, wiped out by the Caul. "So tell me. What do you do every day of your life?"

"I try to do what would be right if I had no power at all," said Quinza, and then she let go of his hand and left him there without saying another word.

CHAPTER 7

JUNGLEWORLD

THE FLYING BEASTS KEPT COMING, PLUNGING THROUGH THE jungle canopy one after another. No sooner had Tork cut the screaming reptilian head off one, than another leaped toward him with maw cranked open and cobalt fangs glistening.

He slashed the battleaxe in all directions, its crackling electric blade slicing through tough black hides like a hot knife through snow. Gouts of silver blood exploded from each beast's wounds, spattering the axe and nearby vegetation—then congealing into animate threads and globs that snapped and nipped with snarling ferocity.

Sweat coated Angar's skin as the battle raged on in the high heat of midday, the jungle cooking him as it steamed under the blistering light of the red sun. A moment's rest would replenish him, given him fresh resolve and renewed power—but the dragons continued their bombardment without respite, swooping down endlessly as if from a limitless flock.

Meanwhile, his only possible backup was engaged in a fight of his own on a different level. As Tork battled creatures from above, Rogg grappled with those from below—a swarm of little monsters that looked half-scorpion, half-centipede. As blocky and low to the ground as he was, he was best equipped to stomp and swat the scorpiopedes, crushing them with his heavy feet and snapping them in pieces as if he were breaking twigs in his four obsidian fists.

He was doing great until reinforcements arrived, scuttling over the muddy jungle floor with claws clacking and barbed tails flicking. Dozens flowed toward him in that next wave, and dozens more in the wave after that. Only when Tork slammed a dead dragon into their midst did the advancing army scatter, at least momentarily.

"So much for this being a safe route across the valley!" shouted Tork as another dragon shot toward him, screeching. "I thought you *knew* this trail!"

"And I thought *you* knew this whole world's in *constant* flux!" said Rogg. "Which should be *obvious* if you've *lived* here more than five minutes!"

As Tork hacked at the dragon, lopping off its head, a phalanx of scorpiopedes charged Rogg from between the scaly corpses of the beasts who'd preceded it. Their tail stingers tagged Rogg again and again as he squashed them with pounding stomps, but the stings had no effect on his dense and thick-skinned form.

"These things never *stop!*" Just as Tork tossed away his

latest kill, another dragon hurtled toward him, filling the jungle with the loudest shrieks yet. "As fast as I kill them, more attack!"

"Maybe...maybe I can help." Rogg crushed another division of scorpiopedes underfoot, then clasped all four hands overhead and closed his ruby red eyes. Instantly, his body glowed with a throbbing yellow aura that expanded with each rhythmic pulse.

"Rogg?" asked Tork as he chopped off another dragon's head and flung the dying body to the ground.

But Rogg was too caught up in his transformation to answer. The yellow light flared, consuming him, and briefly blinded Tork in the bargain.

Moments later, Tork's sight returned, but he didn't see Rogg at his feet anymore. Blinking away the spots in his eyes, Tork looked right, then left, but saw only more dragons diving toward him and scorpiopedes on the march.

Then, he heard a voice from above and looked up.

"It happened again!" The voice was wavery and high-pitched, not at all like Rogg's...or was it? "My change was disrupted!"

The voice came from a bright red sphere that was drifting among the jungle trees, a pair of eyes like hard-boiled eggs with blackened yolks for pupils emblazoned on its glossy surface.

Stunned, Tork stared up at the sphere, watching it bump between trees on an errant breeze. He'd seen Rogg change shape before, it wasn't a total shock—but the shape itself was. He'd never seen anything quite like that redskinned sphere that was floating above him, lighter than air. It was almost beautiful, the way it drifted on errant breezes, gracefully bobbing along.

Then, suddenly, another dragon punched through the canopy and made contact, sending the sphere careening among the treetops.

Tork had to look away, focus his attention on the latest battle...but he still heard Rogg's new voice howling. "Yaggghhh!" Whatever he'd become, he wasn't faring well in that new state.

Grunting with exertion, Tork tore into the latest dragon, splitting open its belly with the axe. Its guts spilled out, squirming and biting with independent life as soon as they cleared the body cavity.

It took several more slashes to incapacitate the thing and hack the life out of its innards and fluids. By then, Rogg had worked his way back to hover overhead once more.

"This is what the invaders' Song does to us!" he said. "It's not much good being a shapeshifter if you can't control the form you take!"

"So shift again!" hollered Tork as yet another dragon lunged down at him. "Try another form!"

"I'm trying!" said Rogg. "It takes time, especially with that *dixnay* signal constantly blasting away!"

Tork didn't mention that he couldn't hear it himself. He was too busy goring the latest dragon with the spike of the axe, then driving it down into the throng of scorpiopedes stinging his legs with painful poison.

As the squealing creatures scattered in a clatter of claws and tails, the yellow light of transformation blazed, blinding him again. As soon as his vision cleared, he looked for Rogg in his new form, which for a moment he couldn't find.

Suddenly, he was distracted by another assault from above—three dragons this time, bigger than any of the others he'd fought. They blasted toward him, their screeches like deafening sirens, their mighty wings plastered to their sides for the streamlined dive.

Tork steeled himself, raising the axe. The beasts flashed downward, fangs gleaming, claws outstretched. He wasn't sure he could take all three of them at once, especially with the scorpiopedes resuming their attack from below.

"Come on, you pieces of *shang.*" He hissed the words between clenched teeth, tightening his grip on the handle of the axe.

Then, without warning, something rocketed out from between the trees and plowed into them, propelling them away from Tork.

The three dragons crashed into a cluster of trees so hard, two of them snapped and splintered. As soon as they hit, the figure that had thrown them there leaped away, landing near Tork with such force, its huge webbed feet squashed dozens of scorpiopedes.

"*This* shape's a bit more useful, wouldn't you say?" said the figure, which looked like a kind of furry purple frog, bigger than Tork himself. "Sometimes it all works out!"

"Move, Rogg!" Tork swung his axe overhead and released it. Just as Rogg sprang to one side, the crackling blade spun past him and landed in the torso of a dragon about to launch itself at Tork.

The beast split apart in a burst of squirming silver goo

that hit the surrounding ground and vegetation and wriggled away in all directions.

"Nice job, Rogg." Tork jogged over to retrieve the axe from the dragon's remains. "You're not bad in a fight, you know that?"

Rogg squatted in the mud and let out a loud, resounding croak. "You're not bad yourself, barbarian."

Finally, there was a moment's peace, free of aerial attackers. The scorpiopedes, however, were another story. They soon regrouped and merged into a huge composite creature that flailed its dozens of legs as it roared at the sky.

"Looks like we're not done yet." Tork gripped the handle of the axe with both hands, ready for the fight to resume.

"No problem, partner." Rogg croaked again. "We'll mop that thing up in no time at all."

"Good, because we need to get moving," said Tork. "This is only day one of our journey. If *every* day is like *this*, we're *never* going to get where we're going."

CHAPTER 8

HELLCYON

T-MINUS TEN HOURS AND COUNTING.

That was the latest announcement over the shipwide intercom as Angar approached the door of his quarters. There were just ten hours until the *Hellcyon* set out for Caul space on the trail of Tork.

It was more than enough time for Angar to get some sleep...and he knew he needed it. He'd been working nonstop for days on a handful of catnaps, trying to train and unify the Hordespeople before they landed in the middle of enemy space.

But when the door dissolved and he stepped through, he quickly realized that sleep might not be in the cards. The three angry women who were waiting for him—his wives—didn't look like they were there to help him catch up on his rest.

"Angar!" Vixa, with her long black hair, was the first to storm toward him, wagging her index finger. "How *could* you side with the Easterners against us?"

Angar glared silently, stopping in his tracks.

"Yes, Angar!" Redheaded Peri stepped up next, arms folded across her chest. "If I didn't know any better, I might think you're nothing but the Blacksmiths' lackey!"

Again, Angar didn't answer.

His other wife, Reyel, just stood back with a baby balanced on each hip, their chubby hands tangled in her long, blonde hair. "I thought you had *plans*, Angar. I thought you had *ambition.*"

"*Enough!*" Not for the first time, Angar found himself wondering why he'd ever married the three women. He wondered, also, why he'd asked the Blacksmiths to include them among the recruits they'd brought aboard the ship.

At first, they'd been too shocked to get into trouble— too overwhelmed by the avalanche of revelations and information that had inundated Angar and Tork before them. They'd been too busy learning about space and starships and alien beings and the Caul to come up with ways to torment their husband.

Unfortunately, they were fast learners. Angar wouldn't have minded if it had taken them months to adjust—but they'd settled in much faster, and the peace and quiet were gone. The three wives were on a perpetual tear, and letting him off the hook wasn't part of their game.

"Listen, Horde Lord." Peri sidled up to him, eyes narrowed seductively. "I know you brought the Hordes here so you could put them to work for us. This incredible ship and all its power should be yours."

He didn't bother answering. She was only partly correct.

"But what if you wait too long to make your move?" asked Peri. "You've said it yourself—this ship might not survive its next mission."

"Then what?" snapped Reyel. "Then you've got *nothing*, not even your *life* or any of *ours*,"

"Even if we *do* survive, you've got a problem." Vixa gave her long black hair a defiant toss. "Those *Easterners* might take control before *you* do."

As Angar listened, he wondered if the Blacksmiths had implanted controllers in his wives' heads as they had in his and Tork's. Would Finn Gauge loan him the remote control if he asked nicely?

"The Easterners are the least of our problems," said Angar. "Without their lord, they fall into line."

"Until you bring him back to them!" shouted Vixa. "Like a good dog on your masters' leash!"

"Or are your promises to the Blacksmiths all deception?" asked Peri. "A way to fool them until you're ready to pounce?"

"Lies can be the greatest weapons of all, my husband!" said Reyel. As if in agreement, the babies on her hips chose that moment to start bawling their lungs out.

Suddenly, Angar had had enough. "Shut up, all of you!" It didn't take much to channel his rage into an outburst. "I've heard enough!"

The women and babies fell silent, though he could tell it wouldn't last. It never did.

"You are to *trust* and *obey* me in all things, are you not? That is the *vow* that you took!" As he glared around the room, no one argued the point. "You are sworn to *accept* my actions as husband and Horde Lord, even if my full intentions are not made plain to you at first!"

Again, no one else in the room spoke.

"Then *trust* me when I tell you that all is in readiness," said Angar. "When the time is right, the signal will be given…and you will *understand*."

"Understand what?" Vixa didn't look or sound convinced.

"In the meantime, do as you're *told*," said Angar. "There are *reasons* for everything, and they will soon be made clear!"

"I have a better idea," said Vixa. "Give me the Eastern Horde."

Angar scowled. "What?"

"Put me in charge of them, and I will make *sure* they fall in line." Vixa sneered. "They will *eagerly* obey your will."

Angar met her gaze. He towered over her, could easily break her, yet she dared challenge him. She dared ask for something she knew he would never give—command of a power that could rival his own.

Unless, as he suspected, she had a control implant in her head…in which case, neither of them was a true threat to each other or the Blacksmiths.

"You get nothing," he told her. "And if you're not careful, I'll move you from *first* among my wives to *last*."

With a furious grunt, she punched him in the chest. "*Shang-hole!*" Then, she stormed out of the quarters and disappeared into the corridor without looking back.

Satisfied for the moment, he whirled on the other two,

who'd backed away. Without Vixa in the mix, they were never as bold, never as likely to rebel.

Not that that had been much of a problem before they'd left Earth. The dangers and rewards of their new reality had unsettled them, thrown off the balance of power in the relationship. The *Hellcyon* was a pressure cooker for Hordespeople who were more accustomed to playing out their dramas in the vast wastelands of their homeworld.

"Anyone else?" Angar looked from Peri to Reyel and back. Neither looked happy, but both shook their heads in the end. "Good. Then let me get to bed while I can. I need sleep, and I have barely enough time for it now."

He marched forward, and they parted, allowing him to pass through into the bedroom. Peri hesitated, then followed him in.

The bedroom door materialized behind them, solid and soundproof and safe.

CHAPTER 9

JUNGLEWORLD

TORK WAS DRENCHED WITH SWEAT AS HE TRUDGED ACROSS the swamp in the afternoon heat and humidity. He moved more slowly than usual, rationing his energy—staying alert for attacks by savage wildlife at any moment.

If it wasn't the hottest day he'd experienced since coming to Jungleworld, it was close enough. It was the kind of heat that could wear down even a warrior hordesman in the best of physical shape, making him wonder how much longer he could go without stopping or passing out.

Not that it seemed to bother Rogg. The shapeshifter had reverted to his squat obsidian form, which for some reason seemed well adjusted to the heat and humidity. He just kept splashing along through the murky water that was up over his knees, humming when he wasn't busy talking to Tork…or himself.

He talked to himself a lot, actually. Tork noticed it over and over again, though he couldn't understand whatever language he was using. Sometimes, he thought the little creature was carrying on a conversation with himself, exchanging comments back and forth in two different voices. It was possible, he thought…especially since the shapeshifter was capable of taking on multiple physical forms. Maybe he had multiple personalities as well.

If he did, Tork sometimes wished he would switch to a different one.

"Come on, Victim Eater." Rogg was out ahead, gesturing with all four hands for Tork to catch up. "We've got a long, long way to go."

I don't eat my victims. Tork had already corrected him numerous times and didn't bother saying it again. "How far, exactly?"

"*Very.*" Rogg laughed. "*Extremely* very."

"But what is the actual distance from here to there?"

"How should I know?" asked Rogg. "Do I look like a map to you?"

Tork thought about taking a swing with his battleaxe… just to get Rogg's attention, of course. "If you don't know the *distance,* can you at least tell me the *time?* How many hours or days will it take to get there?"

"Let me think." A snakelike creature with three heads and a coat of slime-soaked violet feathers reared out of the water before Rogg. With surprising speed, he lashed out one craggy black hand and grabbed it by the throat— then snapped the throat easily and flicked the dead thing away. "By your measure, I would say it will take two weeks."

"Two weeks?" Tork couldn't keep the disappointment out of his voice.

"Wait." Rogg looked back at him. "Weeks are the longer ones, right? Isn't that what you said? Not months."

Tork shook his head. "Months are four times longer."

"Then that's the one." Rogg smiled and nodded. "Or is it years?"

"*Years?*"

"Hey, it's a big planet, all right?" Rogg shrugged. "But no, it was definitely months." He turned and kept slogging through the swamp. "I'm almost completely sure of it."

Just then, something swam past them—a bright red creature with jagged spines down its back and tail, as long as three Torks lined up head to foot to head. The tip of its sinuous tail brushed against Tork's legs, triggering him to instantly draw his axe and hit the contact that switched on the power.

He held still, ready for the great beast to double back and attack. Hacking apart a monster wouldn't be a bad thing, given his current frame of mind.

But the sunken giant just drifted off among the knobby trees with their great droopy caps, ignoring its possible prey.

"Now that one you could have eaten," said Rogg. "Those damn things are *delicious,* even *raw.* A real *delicacy.*"

"Thanks for telling me sooner, when I could've still *killed* it," snapped Tork.

"If it didn't kill you first!" Rogg chuckled, which to Tork sounded like chunks of gravel scraping together.

"Well, I'll need to eat *something* soon," said Tork. "I'm starved."

"No problem." Rogg looked from side to side as he kept slogging. "We'll just find you a nice Caul patrol for you to munch on..."

"I was thinking more of a roast *shapeshifter*, to tell you the truth. You can turn into *anything*, can't you?"

"For you, I'll only turn into gristle," said Rogg. "*Poison* gristle."

Tork was ready to say something nasty in reply, but a distant sound caught his attention. Cocking his head, he tried to make it out.

Slowly, it came into focus—a faraway roar, like a downpour of rain blasting the landscape. Without a word, he veered left, heading in the direction of that roar.

It took a few more steps before Rogg realized they'd drifted apart. "Hey!" Splashing like a maniac, he jogged over to rejoin his traveling companion. "What the *shang* has gotten into you?"

"Nothing." Tork gestured as if patting the air behind him, signaling Rogg to quiet down. "Can't you *hear* it?"

Rogg stopped splashing and listened. "The squawking of the carrion birds, you mean? The chittering of the flesh beetles?"

"No, *that*." Tork pointed in the direction of the roar.

"Oh, *that*." Rogg nodded. "You know that's out of our way, right? We'll lose time going to see it."

"It sounds...*huge*." Tork resumed walking. "Whatever it is, I want to see it."

"But I thought this trip is taking too much time for you..."

"Just shut up and come on," said Tork. "Or I may yet develop an appetite for poisonous shapeshifter gristle."

AFTER ANOTHER FEW MILES, THE SWAMP FADED INTO MUDDY grassland—and a mile or two after that, the grassland melted into dense jungle. Every step of the way, the roar grew louder and closer, drawing Tork inexorably forward.

By the time he and Rogg reached the jungle's edge, the roar was almost deafening. Heart racing with anticipation, Tork hurried toward it, slashing his way through the last tangles of vines and snakes with his crackling, sparking axe.

One more swing of the axe, and he emerged from the treeline. A vast space opened up before him, and he finally saw what was making that roar, what had reeled him in from across such a distance.

And it took his breath away.

Forgetting Rogg at his side, forgetting their quest, forgetting everything, he stepped forward and gazed at the glorious sight. Everywhere he looked, torrents of water rushed over towering cliffs, blasting down into vast clouds of roiling white mist.

Stepping closer to the cliff's edge, he gazed deep into the great gulf. There among the hammering falls and billowing mist, a massive rainbow arched, glittering with all the colors he could imagine. Birdlike creatures whirled around it, swooping on wide white wings above the chaos.

Tork was rarely captivated by anything, but those titanic waterfalls gripped him. Rogg was shouting something, but he couldn't hear a word and didn't care what he was saying.

All the waterfalls he'd ever seen in the wastelands of Earth had been puny trickles compared to these. Every so-called scenic vista he'd ever glimpsed had been barren and dull.

For that one moment, that one glimpse of grandeur, Tork was grateful he'd leaped through the portal weeks ago and emerged high above the lush green treetops of Jungleworld. Every bit of struggle since then had been worth it, from seizing control of a fighter and riding it to the surface to slaughtering killer beasts and Caul warriors on a daily basis to stay alive. All of that, as grueling as it was, had brought him here, to see something that stirred his soul and made the hairs stand up on the back of his neck.

He knew, without a doubt, that he would never forget it as long as he lived.

Though when Rogg tugged his arm and pointed one stony finger downriver from the waterfalls, he realized that might not be as long as he'd expected.

In the distant sky above that raging river, a dozen Caul drones approached, each sleek silver fighter rocketing toward the falls—and Tork and Rogg—at blistering speed.

CHAPTER 10

HELLCYON

T-MINUS ONE HOUR AND COUNTING.

Just as that latest announcement piped over the intercom, the door to the Cortex—control center of the *Hellcyon*—dissolved to reveal Angar looming in the corridor. He marched in, scowling because he hadn't gotten nearly enough sleep.

"Angar." Finn Gauge waved him over to the central zone of the busy place. "Over here."

People and aliens of every color and shape hurried everywhere at once over the transparent floor, prepping the ship for launch...but they parted without hesitation as Angar approached. He was a towering figure with a commanding presence, impossible to disregard; not to mention, most of them had trained with him and knew what he could do when provoked.

Whatever their motivation, it suited him well that they deferred to him. It was almost as if they'd forgotten the implanted device that kept him under their control, paralyzing him if he became too much of a threat.

Though Angar himself *never* forgot that implant was inside him...or who had *put* it there.

"Ready for action, Horde Lord?" Gauge smiled grimly.

"Always." Angar snorted and curled his thick fingers into fists.

"Let's do another directional check for good measure." Gauge nodded at his chief helmsman and navigator, Lt. Eshe Jelani, who was standing nearby. "Make sure we're headed the right way."

Jelani strode over, smiling, a silver control board cradled in her dark brown hands. "Ready, Horde Lord?"

Angar glared. Another directional check was the last thing he wanted to do. He would have much rather spent the last hour before launch with Quinza Acquiesce in the Skull of the *Hellcyon*.

But he knew he had to cooperate. The whole point of the mission was retrieving Tork, and only Angar could sense his location.

"Get it over with." He leaned down, his long black hair falling around his face. It made him uncomfortable bowing like that, made him feel vulnerable. He had come to trust Jelani and her device, but he still hated it every time she used it on him.

Smoothly, she slipped a thin black band around his head, then touched keys on her control board. The band tingled slightly as she activated it, and the tingling spread through the inside of his head.

Then, all at once, the tingling stopped. His head seemed to disappear, and his mind expanded into the star-filled space beyond the ship.

"Connection achieved." Jelani continued to play the controls on the board. "Remote viewing engaged. Vital signs synchronized."

"Excellent," said Gauge. "Put up the mind's-eye window."

From experience, Angar knew what came next. At the touch of a key, a three-dimensional view of a region of space would appear in midair, a miniature representation of the starfield he now envisioned.

"Simulation achieved," said Jelani.

"Begin rotation," said Gauge.

Angar felt as if he were afloat in space with no ship around him, turning slowly. He reached out, feeling for a trace of Tork's familiar signal.

And then he caught it.

"Stop!" He jolted, bumping the control board out of Jelani's hands. "That's it!"

She grabbed the board from the floor and tweaked the controls. "Heart rate and respiration rising. Directional suggested."

"That way!" said Angar. "I can feel it!"

"Straightline heading attained," said Jelani. "Directional confirmed."

"Well done," said Gauge. "Any variation from prior readings?"

"No sir," said Jelani.

"Get it into the nav computer and replot our course one last time," said Gauge. "Convert straightline to actual and lock it down."

"Will do, sir," said Jelani.

"Thank you, Angar," said Gauge. "Fine work, as always."

Angar heard him, but the words didn't register. He still felt as if he were floating outside, gazing into the twinkling glory of the galaxy.

"Eshe, deactivate simulation. End connection."

Even as Gauge said it, Angar remained adrift in his blissful state, the life-force of his enemy tugging at him like a line, pulling him forward. Where exactly the line ended, he couldn't say, he couldn't see that far—but he knew who waited there, and he knew he was alive.

He felt as if he could just sail all the way out to him, if only the Blacksmiths would let him. He *wanted* to go, wanted to fly through the glittering blackness with nothing and no one holding him back.

He could do it, too, he thought. He was *made* to travel that way. He wouldn't even have trouble breathing, he'd proved that on Io.

What else can you do that you couldn't do before? That was what Quinza had asked him earlier in the Skull.

And one other question, as well. *What will you do with these powers?*

Maybe, he thought, it was time he came up with some answers.

GAUGE STUCK TWO FINGERS IN HIS MOUTH AND LET OUT A shrill whistle. Everyone in the Cortex stopped what they were doing and turned their attention on him.

"It's time, people!" said Gauge. "Once again, we are about to set out on a mission that will likely challenge us in every possible way! A mission to strike a blow against the destructive force that we of The Undoing have sworn to annihilate!"

Everyone cheered and applauded except Angar, who was still a little out of it after the directional. He slouched against the wall and glowered, ignoring Dr. Mode as she ran a scanner over him to check his condition.

"We are ready!" shouted Gauge. "We were tested on Io, and we showed our might! We have trained with the greatest fighters of the Grand and Glorious Horde, and we are stronger than ever!

"Best of all, we have the righteous courage of the vanquished behind us! The spirit of the *trillions* who were wiped out or conquered by the Caul! They cry out for vengeance, they cry out for justice, and *we* The Undoing will deliver it for them!"

Everyone in the Cortex roared and pumped their fists with approval. They stomped their feet and howled, letting loose a battle cry of great ferocity.

It was enough to make Angar look around with fresh appreciation. Something had changed, he noticed. Blood ran hot in the Cortex; a streak of unbridled savagery seemed to be threading its way through the normally cool and peace-loving crew.

"Prepare for launch!" shouted Gauge. "Prepare to crush the Caul!"

Again, the Cortex rocked with furious energy. Angar smiled to himself, because he and Tork had done well in bringing it out of those docile people.

He only hoped they'd taught them how to fight well enough to back up their new bravado on the battlefield... and avoid another Io.

T-minus ten minutes and counting.

"Are you ready for the fun to begin?"

Angar looked left with a start and saw Punji's mottled indigo blossom gazing back at him. Somehow, the Gog plant-man had managed to sneak up on the Horde Lord.

"Are *you* ready?" asked Angar with a smirk.

"I'm the one person on this ship other than you who was never *not* ready." The velvety black nozzle in the heard of Punji's flower head squirmed. "Unlike the humans, my people *never* our warlike ways."

"Yet none of you could stand against the Caul," said Angar. "What makes you think *this* time will be any different?"

Punji's petals rustled as if a stiff breeze were passing. "Because there was never a *horde lord* on our side before." Punji made a chuckling sound in his thick green stalk-throat. "That said, I have just one suggestion for you before we embark on this daring adventure."

"What is that?" asked Angar.

"When you first encounter the Caul face to face," said Punji, "and you finally get to take their measure in the flesh...try not to scream like a little girl."

Angar's face clouded. If he'd thought he could get away with it without being paralyzed by his implant, he would have lashed out and struck the vegetable with staggering force.

"I'm dead serious," said Punji. "You don't know what

you're going up against. You don't know what they're really like."

"*Shang* you," hissed Angar between clenched teeth. "*Nothing* will make *me* scream like a…"

Punji's face pushed closer, and his petals curled. "There's a *reason* the Caul have conquered so much of the galaxy, Angar Crux…and it is *not* because every living being is a weak coward, unlike you."

With that, Punji's flower head zipped away, and he strutted off through the crowd in the Cortex with that rhythmic bob-and-weave stride of his.

That left Angar at the wall, glaring, wishing he'd said the hell with the implant and taken a swing at the plant-man anyway. A Horde Lord would *never* react with fear in *any* circumstance. *No* enemy could inspire the faintest hint of cowardice in his breast.

So why did Punji's words stay with him like a prickly burr stuck in his flesh?

CHAPTER 11

JUNGLEWORLD

"THERE GOES ANOTHER ONE." AT THE SOUND OF A HIGH-
pitched whine coming closer, Tork looked up at a patch of
bright, sunny sky through the overhanging emerald
canopy.

"Another drone," said Rogg. "You can tell by the altitude. Robot drones run lower than manned craft, since
they have no pilots at risk."

"Right." As Tork watched, a silver needle of a ship
crossed the open patch of sky and kept going, the whine
of its engine approaching, then fading with distance. It
was the twelfth drone they'd spotted that day, passing by
on patrol for the Caul. Manned ships were less common
over Jungleworld, and it seemed like he'd *never* see one
now that he'd decided he wanted one.

"You need to relax, big fella," said Rogg as they

continued through the jungle, heading toward the distant source of the "Song" that plagued his people. "Enjoy the journey. Ship or no ship, you'll reach the same destination eventually."

"Two months *later* on foot," snapped Tork. "And who *knows* what the Caul might do by the time we finally get there?"

"Listen," said Rogg. "No one wants to shut down the Song sooner than I do, but if getting a manned Caul ship was possible, don't you think I would've done it by now?"

Tork wasn't so sure, given the shapeshifter's problems with choosing the right form in the middle of a fight. A battle-hardened Horde Lord with a powered-up battleaxe might be able to succeed where the imperfect shifter could not.

"We need to find the nearest flight center," said Tork. "Then ambush a ship when it lands."

"Good luck with that." Rogg grabbed a winged insect as big as his hand, shoved it into his mouth, and gulped it down. "For one thing, those centers are well-hidden and protected. For another thing, the pilots are almost all Cossitora. Total unbeatable maniacs."

Again, Tork thought a Horde Lord might fare better than a scrambled shifter. "And you say you don't know the closest flight center location?"

"Correct," said Rogg.

"Then we keep watching for a manned ship and follow it," said Tork. "Watch where it's going and head in that direction."

"Not so easy in a jungle, barbarian," said Rogg. "And what if they change direction? Or the flight center is hundreds of miles away? Do you know what the range on those ships is? Because I don't."

Tork shrugged. "We need to start somewhere."

"And there's one other thing," said Rogg. "Can you even *fly* one of those things?"

"Can you?"

"Shapeshifters aren't known for their piloting skills," said Rogg. "We usually just grow wings and do the flying ourselves...when we aren't disrupted by a stupid Song, that is."

"Don't worry." Tork reached down and patted him on the head. "We'll figure it out."

Even as he said it, though, he had his doubts. He'd flown in a fighter with Valla Viss at the Battle of Io, had seen her work the controls of the Blacksmith ship...but he hadn't piloted the ship himself. Even if he could have, he doubted the controls of the Caul ships would be the same.

Still, if there was any kind of chance that he could reach the Song source and free Rogg's people sooner, he had to take it. Not to mention, a captured ship might come in handy in other ways, too.

"I'm starting to think you're crazier than I thought," said Rogg. "Which I guess shouldn't be a surprise, as much killing as you've done around here, but..."

"Shhh!" Tork cocked his head and listened. He heard the distinct whine of an approaching engine, somewhere far above. "There's another one."

Trotting ahead, he found an open patch of canopy and fixed his gaze on the bright blue sky beyond. This time, the passing ship was different in shape—a gold wedge instead of a silver needle—and clearly flying at a higher altitude than those he'd seen before.

Rogg also watched it pass and nodded slowly. "Could be, could be..."

"I've got a feeling about that one," said Tork. "Let's go."

With that, he started running through the jungle, glancing up every few steps to make sure he was keeping pace with the ship.

Rogg just sighed and scurried after him, fighting to keep up as best he could.

CHAPTER 12

HELLCYON

THE *HELLCYON* LEAPED INTO RIP SPACE, ROCKETING ALONG on a course that Angar had helped plot. Streamers of rainbow light flowed all around the ship, rippling and mingling with the blazing red exhaust beams pouring out of its tailpipes.

Angar himself was conscious the whole time, which was a mark of progress for him. The first time he'd experienced the Rip Drive, he'd ended up blacking out and collapsing on the floor of the Cortex—but he'd finally gotten used to the ship's mode of travel through space. He also knew better now than to refuse to strap into a launch seat when a Rip countdown started.

Just knowing what a Rip Drive was (if not exactly how it worked) showed how far he'd come from his days of ignorance and strife back home. He hadn't even known

ROBERT JESCHONEK

what space was back then, or that it was possible to travel through it. Now he was out there among the stars himself, hurtling forth at impossible speeds.

Though it was true that the strife was still with him on a scale he could never have imagined before.

"All right everyone." Gauge unsnapped the harness on his command chair and got to his feet. "The *Hellcyon* is underway. We expect to reach our destination in approximately 48 hours."

Across the Cortex, crew members undid their restraints and went back to work, hurrying in all directions with control boards and other devices in hand.

"In the meantime, round-the-clock battle drills are in effect," said Gauge. "I want us at full readiness the instant we drop out of Rip Space."

"Aye, sir!" Punji glided to the middle of the Cortex and raised his voice over the hubbub of the crew for attention. "All team leaders, reference drill 01-Alpha-Caul in your Ready Book." The fronds of his fingers flicked over the silver control board he held, and columns of glowing red text appeared in midair before him. "You have five minutes to ready your teams and stations!"

Unhooking his own launch harness, Angar rose from his seat and headed for the door. Checking on the people of the hordes was his next priority.

Before he could make it out of the Cortex, however, Isabel Haussman cut him off. "The natives are restless," she said coolly, her green-eyed gaze locked on his face.

Angar frowned. "Natives?"

"The hordes," said Isabel. "Something's up. Something has changed."

"What makes you think that?" asked Angar.

"Rumors and intuition." Isabel nodded. "Plus algorithmic analyses of their movements and interactions."

Angar had no idea what algorithmic analysis was. "You've been spying on them?"

"Somewhat," said Isabel.

Angar smirked. "Well, I can guarantee you're only seeing and hearing what they *want* you to."

"Perhaps *you* might find out more," said Isabel. "And offer some insight."

"There is no need," said Angar. "My people do as they must to prepare for the coming crucible. Don't waste your time reading things into their comings and goings."

"We're depending on them." Isabel's gaze held a steely glint. "If we can't, for some reason, we need to change our plans."

"Leave them to me." Angar nodded. "Worry about the readiness of *your own* people instead."

"Take a look anyway, Horde Lord," she told him. "Remember, it's *your* life on the line as well as ours if this goes sideways."

"How lucky for you that we aren't back on Earth in my kingdom." Angar leaned close, his black hair swinging toward her face. "Otherwise, you might now be dead for daring to take that tone with me."

Isabel snorted, unafraid. "Says the man with bomb in his head." She waved a silver control board at him. "And my finger on the button."

Then, leaving her last words hanging in his mind, she turned and walked away, the control board hanging loosely at her side.

~

WHEN ANGAR MARCHED INTO THE HANGAR DECK, HE stopped in his tracks and took in the scene that played out before him.

A great battle was unfolding throughout the vast space —all-out, hand-to-hand combat between dozens of fighters. The chamber rang with shouts and cries and crashes as men and women clashed, battering each other furiously with fists and feet and knees and skulls.

In some cases, the fights were one on one. In others, two or more people went up against one, slamming them into submission with force of numbers.

In all cases, though, the results were the same. People of the hordes were dominating members of the ship's crew, mowing them down again and again. It wasn't even a contest.

The crew fought hard, but they were outnumbered and overpowered. It was only a matter of time until the tougher and more experienced fighters of the hordes subdued every one of them.

As Angar watched, a dark feeling welled up within him. In spite of all the training he and Tork had tried to give, he realized the *Hellcyon*'s crew could never overcome the brutal Caul on their own. As hard as they tried, they were nowhere near ready yet. The suffering and losses at the Battle of Io had hardened them some, but not enough.

It made him so angry, he wanted to get into the mix and pummel the crew-people himself, to teach them a lesson.

But then, Major Schist strode out of the heart of the

melee and hollered loud enough to be heard over the chaos.

"*Stop!* Exercise over!"

Not everyone stopped fighting at once, but the brawl did start to wind down. The punches and kicks stopped flying, the angry shouts quieted, and the people straightened and dusted themselves off.

For a moment, then, a stark tableau confronted Angar, an ominous, haunting vision: dozens of *Hellcyon* crew on the floor, defeated, as the people of the hordes stood over them.

"Take five, everyone!" ordered Schist. "We'll resume with close-quarters weapons practice!"

He turned, then, and marched over to greet Angar. "Horde Lord, welcome! Care to join the next drill?"

Angar shook his head. "Impressive, Schist. I can't believe the Eastern and Southern hordes are working together here against a common opponent."

Schist's crystalline face turned lavender, the color of gratitude for his mineral-based species. "You should have seen the drill before this one! The Easterners were working with the crew against the Southerners! Hell of a dust-up!"

"As I said, impressive." Angar grinned.

"So are you hear to observe, or do you want to get in there and do a little sparring?" Schist aimed a flurry of punches at the air.

"Actually, I have a request," said Angar. "I need you to stay alert for signs of trouble among the hordespeople."

"That's a tall order." Schist's crystalline form changed color to pink for irritation. "There's *always* conflict between our new recruits. The Easterners and South-erners are blood enemies, so..."

"There are rumors that's something's in the wind," said Angar. "That something bad it coming, and it's starting with someone here." He gestured at the crowd milling around the hangar.

"No details beyond that?" asked Schist.

Angar shook his head. "We can't afford trouble from within right now. We've got enough conflict as it is, going after Tork in Caul territory."

"I'll do what I can." Schist scanned the crowded chamber as if searching for danger signs. "The hordes-people don't exactly confide in me, you know. There's a saying: they play their cards close to their vests."

"Just do your best." Even as he said it, Angar knew that what he was asking was pretty hopeless. When hordes-people closed ranks, their wall of silence could not be broken.

But just surrendering, not making any effort at all to head off whatever storm might be coming, wasn't some-thing he could bring himself to do. *That* was not the way of a true Horde Lord.

"You might have better luck than I will," said Schist. "Especially with the Southern Horde."

"You might be surprised." Angar smirked. "Some Southerners think I should have left them back home instead of dragging them into someone else's war." Angar took a deep breath and let it out slowly. "Sometimes, I think the same thing."

Schist, whose inner light had turned the bright green of affection, reached over and patted Angar's shoulder. "I don't. The Undoing can't defeat the Caul on their own. We need your people to help us...and inspire us with the courage we've lacked."

Angar nodded. "Thank you, my friend." He patted Schist's shoulder in return. "And please, watch your back."

"Will do." With that, the crystalline man changed from green to red and turned to resume yelling at the crew and hordespeople, spinning up the next round of hand-to-hand combat.

CHAPTER 13

JUNGLEWORLD

RUNNING THROUGH THE JUNGLE WHILE TRYING TO FOLLOW a ship in flight hadn't been such a great idea. Tork had had to dodge one obstacle after another, from beasts to branches to rocks to quicksand, all while barely keeping the golden wedge of the ship in sight overhead.

As for Rogg, he'd gotten the worst part of the deal by far. In his stumpy, obsidian form, he'd had a lot more trouble clearing obstacles and couldn't keep up with Tork. He changed shape but ended up as an airborne manta with poor eyesight and kept slamming into trees. He caught up a little when he shapeshifted again, becoming a kind of living stream of bubbles that squirted its way through the dense foliage—but that turned out to be not so great, too, when iridescent hummingbirds darted over to pop those bubbles with their needle-like beaks. Changing back to his rocky self, he hit the ground running, hoping to catch sight of Tork just as Tork was hoping to catch sight of the ship's flight center.

Scrambling out of the thickest patch of undergrowth ever, Rogg got his wish. There on the edge of a cliff, Tork stood and gazed, shading his eyes against the blazing red sun.

"Hey!" Rogg tore away the last clinging tangles of brush and stumbled over to join him. "Did you lose it? The ship?"

Tork raised an arm and extended an index finger, pointing into the distance. "There."

Rogg followed his gaze and saw it—the golden ship slowly descending, coming in for a graceful landing in a jungle clearing. Best of all, at the far end of the clearing, mostly concealed by jungle foliage, was a boxy silver building—low to the ground yet sprawling, big enough to serve as a hangar and maintenance facility for multiple ships.

"Flight center," said Rogg. "You found one after all. Good for you."

"Now we just need to get down there and take that ship before it launches again." Tork looked over the edge of the cliff as if considering a leap to the bottom. "Too bad your shape-changes are so unpredictable. It would be nice to fly down on the back of a dragon or something."

"Tell me about it." Rogg sounded wistful. "I can think of a dozen creatures off the top of my head that would be perfect for getting us down there."

Without further hesitation, Tork started jogging along the edge of the cliff, looking for a good place to start down. The cliff wasn't sheer; if he could find the right spot, he figured he could make the climb just fine.

Sure enough, Tork quickly found a section of cliff that had ample handholds and ledges that looked solid from afar. Strapping his sword to his back, he crouched and lowered himself over the edge, beginning his climb down.

Rogg stood on the rim and watched him go. "What about me?"

"Can you turn into a bug? Something small enough to ride me down?"

Rogg concentrated, fighting the effects of the Song that still played in his mind. He focused all his energy on transforming into an insect, a bug that could hop onto the Horde Lord's shoulder without adding enough weight and mass to disrupt the climb.

Instead, he became a winged beetle that was almost as big as Tork.

Much too big to ride Tork's shoulder, Rogg spread his gleaming black wings and started them fluttering at a high rate of speed. His spindly, clawed feet left the ground, and he leaned forward, angling for the great open chasm beyond the cliff. Feeling lighter than air despite his great size, he buzzed over the rim and started his descent.

"See you downstairs!" he shouted as he passed Tork, who was carefully moving from handhold to handhold, heading for a wide ledge.

But he didn't get far before the sound of the Song in his head got louder and more insistent. He felt his body respond instantly, converting the beetle shape into some-thing else...something less *airborne*.

"Oh no!" Before Rogg could fling himself at the cliff

face in the hope of grabbing hold, his bug-shaped body twisted into a new shape—an armor-plated metallic form with no wings or other means to keep himself aloft.

In that instant, Rogg plummeted toward the ground far below, struggling in vain to transform again and become something lighter and less likely to come down explosively hard.

As for Tork, he just kept steadily, carefully climbing, making plans for what he would do at the flight center when he got there.

WHEN TORK REACHED THE END OF HIS CLIMB AND STEPPED away from the cliff, he saw the crater where Rogg had crashed...but no Rogg. Then, suddenly, the shifter came crashing out of the nearby brush in his obsidian form, eyes flashing a brighter red than usual.

"Come with me! Hurry!" He spun and headed back into the jungle, gesturing for Tork to follow. "Come on!"

Tork swung the battleaxe off his back and ran after Rogg without hesitation. Whatever the cause of the shapeshifter's panic, he would know it soon enough.

"This way!" Rogg bolted through the dense foliage, leaped over trickling streams, and barreled up a muddy hillside. Just as he reached the crest, the high-pitched whine of a weapon pierced the hot, humid air, followed by the screams of living things on the other side of the hill.

Tork scowled as he topped the hill beside Rogg and looked down. There, in a clearing lined with small huts made of fronds and vines and branches, three Narl fired energy-beam rifles at a clutch of fragile-looking, green-skinned creatures with big, bright eyes and bodies that swayed and rippled like flags in a breeze.

"We've got to help them!" Rogg said over the whines of the guns.

Tork balanced the axe in his hands, preparing. "Not the Narl, obviously."

"The green ones! The ones getting shot!" As he said it, another of the big-eyed creatures was hit by a gunshot. The others screamed as he slumped to the ground. "They're *my people!*"

That was all he needed to say. Tork hauled back the axe, powering it up in the process, then flung it forward. It spun through the air and landed square in the broad blue back of a Narl, sending the beast pitching forward.

Even before it hit, Tork was charging down the slope, teeth clenched in a murderous grimace.

The two uninjured Narl swung around with their guns at the ready, howling with rage. Their first shots were wild, and then the rifles didn't matter anymore. Tork hauled the axe out of the dropped Narl's back without breaking stride, then hurled it at one of the Narl who still opposed him, splitting its head open along the line between its ram's horns.

Even as that Narl fell, Tork leaped at the last of the three. Bolts flashed from the creature's gun, all near misses, and Tork crashed into him like a boulder, driving him hard to the ground. His rifle tumbled out of his grip and out of reach, firing one last shot as it bounced.

The beast roared and thrashed, its spines slashing Tork's flesh. Tork wasted no time pounding it with blow after blow, plunging his fists into its head until the face gave way like a rotten apple. He sprang away then, before the Narl's acid could spurt out and burn him, though he came away with a few extra gashes from the beast's spines when he wrenched himself free.

With that, Tork was the last fighter left standing amid the twitching carcasses. Pulling his axe from the split skull of one of the Narl, he wiped the acid and blood from its blade on a leafy bush.

"Thank you," said Rogg, who stood among the big-eyed survivors he'd called his people. "Thank you for saving them, Tork."

Tork grunted. "It wasn't much of a fight." He managed to sound disappointed.

"You did a good thing here, my friend." As Rogg said it, two of the big-eyed creatures pressed their sinuous green bodies against his rocky obsidian form. "The Narl would have slaughtered them all if you hadn't stepped in."

"I'm only sorry we couldn't save all of them." Tork looked at the dead shifters that littered the ground among the Narl.

"We missed two other villages, as well," Rogg said darkly. "The Narl never stop killing our kind. The Caul have ordered them to wipe out every last one of us."

"Why is that?" asked Tork.

"The same reason they broadcast that *Song* to interfere with our abilities," said Rogg. "*Fear.*"

Tork nodded, though he thought the big-eyed creatures didn't look like much of a threat. Neither did Rogg, for that matter.

"The crazy thing is, they're so wrong about us." Rogg

gently stroked the two creatures who were pressed against him. "We never cared about them. We never would have, if they'd left us alone.

"And we could have told them a secret that would have saved them, if they'd stopped killing us long enough to listen."

Tork's eyes narrowed. "What secret is that?"

"We're not the ones they should be scared of," said Rogg. "We're not even close."

CHAPTER 14

HELLCYON

ANGAR WAS IN THE SKULL, WAITING TO MEET AN EASTERN Horde informer, when the *Hellcyon* dropped out of Rip Space.

The change was so sudden, it threw him against the bulkhead. Cursing, he pushed away and gazed out through the ruby eyes of the Skull. Instead of the unfettered chaos of Rip Space with its whirling clouds of multicolored gas and blazing bolts of energy, he saw the star-filled blackness of normal space out there, still and serene.

Except for the massive derelict vessel afloat in the darkness, gashed open and without the slightest twinkle of power.

"What the *shang?*" Instantly, he gave up waiting for the informer, who was late anyway, and charged out of the Skull in search of answers.

He ran to the Cortex and rushed inside, only to find the place was surprisingly quiet. Everyone was focused, in one way or another, on the wrecked ship displayed on the holographic viewer.

"No response to hails, Captain." Culma Doreen, the avian communications officer, followed her report with a high, whistling trill from her post at the far edge of the Cortex. "The distress signal is still the only transmission from the *Echelon.*"

"Keep trying, Lieutenant." Gauge got up from his chair in the middle of the room and walked up for a closer look at the ship on the screen. "Isabel, analysis."

"No life signs." Isabel was busy at the science station, eyes glued to the holographic controls and readouts displayed in midair around her. "No life support. No power except the distress call battery. The *Echelon* is dead in space. She's been that way for at least 24 hours, judging from the residual energy signatures of the weapons that shot her to hell."

"What weapons, specifically?" asked Gauge.

"Quinteri particle beams." Punji was stationed at Tactical, directly behind Gauge's command seat. "Boosted by Caul power arrays, as usual. Poor bastards fought back, but the Caul tech overwhelmed them."

"One less gunship in the fleet," Gauge said darkly.

"And a hundred fewer fighters in the war," added Isabel.

Angar stepped forward then, joining Gauge at the screen. "The enemy's out there, aren't they? Waiting to spring the trap."

"Unknown," said Isabel. "There are signs of Rip engine activity from approximately sixteen hours ago, indicative of a vessel departing the system."

"But they may have doubled back," said Punji. "Popped out of the Rip on the other side of the star and did a zero-burn glide to hide out behind an asteroid."

"In which case, we won't find them until they show themselves," said Isabel. "At which point, they'll have the advantage."

"So how are we going to board the *Echelon* before that happens?" asked Gauge.

"Board the dead ship?" Angar looked at him like he was crazy. "Why the *shang* would we do that?"

"That information is classified." Gauge turned stiffly and made his way to the command chair. "Suffice it to say, a boarding party is needed."

"Do we have *time* for this?" Angar jabbed a finger at the screen. "Tork is still out there somewhere! Every minute we delay puts him more at risk."

"That can't be helped," said Gauge. "There are other imperatives of equal or greater importance."

"More important than saving one of the saviors of the *galaxy?*"

Gauge nodded. "Trust me, it is." He cast a look of grim sincerity at Angar...and then he turned away and barked out a string of orders. "Punji, you're in command. Isabel and Rerox, you're with me."

Isabel smoothly handed off her science station to a waiting crewman. Rerox, who was posted at the security station, also left things in other hands and clomped toward the door. His armor-clad body clanked as he walked, each footfall like the dropping of an anvil.

As Gauge also headed for the door, he tapped his right earlobe, jacking into the comm system. "Commander Viss! Ready a pod! We leave in five minutes."

"Hurry back, Captain," said Punji as he slipped into Gauge's chair. "You wouldn't want us to leave without you."

"Just don't scratch my ship while I'm away," shouted Gauge on his way out the door. "I'll bust your rank all the way back to a seedling, I swear to God."

ANGAR WAS BEYOND PISSED AS HE STOMPED DOWN THE corridor from the Cortex. Not only was Gauge endangering the ship and its mission, but his reason for doing so involved a secret he wouldn't share with the Horde Lord.

Now the *Hellcyon* hung in space like a target, awaiting the wrath of the Quinteri who'd wrecked the *Echelon* or any other passing shipload of hostiles. Even a barbarian who'd never been on a stargoing vessel before knew it was a seriously bad idea.

Based on what The Undoing and Blacksmiths had told him, the fate of the galaxy—and maybe the universe—was riding on the *Hellcyon* and its Horde Lords. How then did it make the slightest bit of sense to risk everything to slip aboard that ruined ship?

It didn't, but that didn't matter. As long as Angar had no real authority, he was helpless to change his fate.

That left him to storm through the corridor, letting

off steam as Gauge and his team flew a transit pod to the shipwreck. It was either that or start smashing things, but he supposed that would be counterproductive.

He headed straight for the Skull—the one part of the ship where he might pull himself together—then stopped in the hall outside when he saw the door was opening and heard voices inside.

"We better get moving."

"They won't be gone long."

Angar flung himself back around the corner and flattened himself against the wall, listening as the two voices approached. Both were muffled by masks pulled over their faces, but Angar could at least tell that one was a man and the other a woman.

"I still hate to move sooner than planned," said the man.

"Captain's off the ship," said the woman. "It would just be *stupid* to pass up such perfect timing."

"What if he gets back early? What do we do then?"

"Hey, think positive," said the woman. "Maybe the Quinteri will show up, and he won't get back at all."

As the two drew near, Angar eased himself away from the corner and into a doorway. He waited there, surprised at what he was hearing—yet not surprised. After all, Isabel had warned him that something was happening among the hordes.

And mutiny was not at all beyond the realm of possibility for his savage people.

"Hey!" Just then, Angar heard running footsteps from the other side of the intersection and a third voice—

young, male, and muffled—fast approaching the other two. "We're all set!"

"That's great," said the woman. "This is going better than I expected."

"That's how it is when Yorg's on your side," said the young man.

"I still say we're moving too fast," said the older man. "We'll have lots of opportunities later, and..."

"Enough!" shouted the woman.

Angar heard her slam the older man against a bulkhead. He got the wind knocked out of him, and then she gave him another slam for good measure.

"Stop being such a coward!" she snapped. "This is happening now whether you like it or not!"

"I'm just trying to be—"

"We don't have time for this!" said the woman, and then she addressed the younger man. "Give me a hand silencing this fool!"

"But we've got to get to the Cortex in five minutes," said the young man.

"So let's make this fast!"

Angar heard more sounds of a struggle, and he knew he had to move. Hiding in a doorway while someone was killed around the corner by mutineers was something he would simply never do.

Stepping out of the doorway, he pulled the sword from its sheath on his back and thumbed the power stud on the grip. Without a word, he marched the few steps to the corner, then turned it with teeth clenched and muscles tight, ready for a fight.

As soon as they saw him, the woman and young man—

both dressed all in black, including full black masks that covered their facial features—charged him as one, leaving their previous victim to slump against the wall.

Angar just smiled and met their charge. It was the best he'd felt all day.

CHAPTER 15

JUNGLEWORLD

TORK AND ROGG SAT ACROSS THE CAMPFIRE FROM EACH other, gazing into the flickering flames. All around them, the jungle screamed with nocturnal life, a wild variety of cries and chirps and roars that echoed through the night.

The two companions had decided to make camp when they'd realized the flight center was farther away on foot than it had looked from the cliff. It would be better to cover the rest of the ground when they were fresh in the morning, more ready to tackle any obstacles that got in their way.

Assuming they could get any sleep in that screeching madhouse of a jungle, that is.

"We should turn in soon." Rogg reached directly into the fire with his rocklike hands and shifted the burning wood. Clearly, the heat didn't bother him at all.

"Good idea." Tork was certainly tired enough to sleep, though he could have kept going if he'd had to. One of the things he'd learned since coming to Jungleworld was that he could go much longer without sleep than he'd imagined. In a place like that, with constant threats on every side, sleep was a luxury he often couldn't afford.

"I'll take first watch, if you want," said Rogg. "I never need a lot of sleep."

"Thanks." Tork yawned. "Nice dinner, by the way."

The charred bones of the lizard they'd eaten were scattered in the fire. Sometime before sundown, Tork had spotted it on a rock, killed it with his axe, and skinned it for Rogg to cook.

"Nice job catching it," said Rogg.

"So what happened to your people?" asked Tork. "They just faded away after we killed the Narl."

"They had to leave. The village wasn't safe anymore."

"So there's some kind of refuge? An underground hiding place like the one where you took me, maybe?"

"Something like that." Rogg shrugged, his obsidian shoulders gleaming in the firelight. "Nowhere's truly safe, though, as long as the Caul and their soldiers are still here."

"So what happens when we stop the Song," asked Tork, "and your people regain control of their shapeshifting? Will they join forces and strike back at the invaders?"

"Wouldn't you?" said Rogg. "Wouldn't you strike back at the people who paralyzed and terrorized you as soon as you got the chance?"

"What about the others?" Tork leaned forward and narrowed his eyes. "The ones you said the Caul should be most scared of? Are they allies? Will your people join forces with them?"

Rogg's ruby eyes met his through the flames, but he didn't answer the question.

Tork opened his mouth to ask it again, then leaned back instead. "So can you find the source of the Song from the air, do you think?" he asked. "Can you guide me there once we get a ship?"

"It's a strong signal," said Rogg. "Impossible to escape if you're a shifter. But then again, I've never flown in one of those ships."

"I'll bet you'll do just fine."

"Something to keep in mind, though," said Rogg. "The closer I get to the source, the stronger the Song becomes...and the more it *hurts*. The biggest problem might be blocking it out, not trying to find it."

Tork stroked his beard and thought for a moment. "Is there anything we can do to limit the pain? Could you take a different form, maybe?"

Rogg shook his head. "Nothing will help that I know of."

"Hmm." Tork frowned. "Maybe I should drop you off before it gets too bad and go in alone."

"I'd like to see you try," said Rogg.

Tork smiled grimly.

"This is *my* war more than yours, barbarian." Rogg reached for another chunk of the firewood that Tork had cut with his axe and pitched in into the flames, making them leap. "And I *will* be there in the belly of the beast when the Song finally falls silent forever."

Tork nodded. If their roles had been reversed, he would have felt the same way.

"All right then." He stretched out beside the fire as the need for sleep rose up in him. "We leave before sunrise. Wake me in a few hours so I can get the second watch."

"Should we talk about a plan?" asked Rogg. "For what you'll do when we get to the flight center?"

"That I won't know until I see the place," said Tork. "But I imagine it will involve a battle of some kind."

"I'm glad you have it all figured out." Rogg shook his head. "I'd hate to think we were going to march in there unprepared."

"I wouldn't dream of it." Some of the nearby creatures paused their cries as he unleashed a long, loud yawn.

"Just remember, I'm relying on you," said Rogg. "All of my people are. You're the last, best chance we have at freedom. Our barbarian from the stars." He chuckled. "Our Starbarian."

Tork's only answer was the first in a long series of blaring snores that rumbled through the jungle like the growls of a great beast prowling the night.

CHAPTER 16

HELLCYON

ANGAR'S SWORD CRACKLED AS HE SWUNG IT AT THE WOMAN and young man who were charging toward him. They both dropped suddenly, leaving the blade to sweep past without touching either of them.

As the sword completed its arc, the two mutineers leaped at Angar, latching onto his upper body. It wasn't until he felt a sudden, sharp pain in his side, however, that he realized one of them was armed with a knife.

Shutting out the pain, Angar flung both fighters off, sending them flying across the corridor. They bounced off the bulkhead and came down hard in a tangled heap on the floor.

Hauling back his sword, Angar advanced, ready to hack the two into submission. Before he could start hack-

ROBERT JESCHONEK

ing, however, someone grabbed him from behind and held on tight around his torso, breaking his stride.

It was the other man, the one the mutineers had been ready to kill just moments ago. He'd forgotten him, assuming he wouldn't fight on their behalf—but somehow, the death threat hadn't been enough to lose his loyalty.

With a roar of rage, Angar tried shaking the man free. He just dug in tighter, refusing to let go.

He grabbed the man's wrist then, and snapped it. Howling, the man released his grip and fell, clutching at the break.

But the distraction had done its job. Just as he whirled to deal with the fighters, an energy beam sizzled past, fired from a pistol held by the woman.

"You should be helping us!" she shouted. "We finally have a chance to control our own destiny!"

Then she fired another blast at Angar. He dove to one side, but the beam still caught his right shoulder, leaving a searing trail of agony.

He hurled his sword then, sending it spinning down the corridor. It knocked the gun free and sent it skittering over the floor, out of her reach...but not far from the young man behind her. He ran for it.

Angar ran, too, intending to swat the woman away and bowl over the young man. Just as he was about to strike her, however, the ship rocked violently.

Angar lost his footing and slammed into a wall instead of the woman. He grabbed for a handrail...and missed when the ship lurched again.

A siren wailed and the lights flickered as he struggled

to stay on his feet. The woman and young man were floundering, too, and ended up falling into each other.

The ship bucked a third time, more violently than ever. This time, the lights stopped flickering, but the gravity went out.

Angar's feet left the floor, and he found himself drifting. The men and woman also lost contact with the floor and floated upward.

For a moment, they all hung suspended, bobbing and turning gently in midair. The woman's dark eyes fixed on him from the eyeholes of the mask, relentless and unafraid.

"Last chance." She made a beckoning gesture. "Join us in taking this ship."

He smirked. "I was just going to say the same thing to you. Last chance to surrender."

She laughed and gave him a middle-finger salute.

It was then that the ship lurched again, sending them all tumbling. The lights went out completely, and the siren went silent.

Angar hit a wall with his wounded shoulder and winced, fighting back the cry of pain that rose in his throat. Staying focused on the fight at hand, he thrust a foot down and hooked his toe on the handrail. The rest of him bumped against the wall and stopped, maintaining position...getting ready to kick off and rocket into the others as soon as the lights came back up.

The gravity came back first, though, and Angar crashed to the floor, striking his head hard on the bulkhead on his way down.

As he slipped into unconsciousness, the lights

returned, too, just in time for him to see the mutineers get back on their feet and run down the corridor.

Only one of them turned and looked back at him, and only for a second—the woman. "This isn't over," she said as she darted away. "You better get your priorities straight before we meet again!"

Angar had to time to consider her words. Darkness welled up within him, dragging him out of the conscious world before he could form another thought.

CHAPTER 17

JUNGLEWORLD

RAIN SLASHED DOWN IN SHEETS AS TORK WATCHED THE flight center entrance from afar. The sun had been up for over an hour, and still the big hangar door remained tightly sealed.

Was it because of the heavy rain that no craft were coming or going? That was Rogg's theory. Or maybe the place was on lockdown because its security systems had detected the interlopers. That also seemed like a strong possibility.

"I'll bet the Narl foot patrols are surrounding us as we speak." Rogg kept his voice low. He and Tork were huddled in thick brush along the runway some 300 yards from the sprawling white building, but discovery was always a possibility when it came to the Caul and their surveillance technology.

"If the Narl come, they'll be quick to die," whispered Tork. "*Anyone* who gets in our way will be quick to die."

"I like what you're saying," said Rogg. "Assuming we don't get killed before we get a ship, I like this whole plan of yours."

"Thank you."

"There's just one little thing that keeps eating at me," said Rogg.

"Other than the voracious jungle ticks?"

"Uh-huh," said Rogg. "You still haven't told me how you plan to fly a ship."

"Sure I have."

"'We'll figure it out' doesn't tell me much," said Rogg.

"Don't worry about it."

"I don't think these Caul ships are so easy to fly that just anyone can do it," said Rogg. "Otherwise, I'm pretty sure *someone* would have stolen them before this and flown them into a Caul installation or something."

Tork finally stopped staring at the building and turned to smile at Rogg. "Do you know how many times I've made things happen that I had no idea how to do?"

Rogg's ruby eyes glinted. "Never?"

"More times than I can remember," said Tork. "And I'll do it again. I'll *improvise*, and it will all work out."

Rogg sighed. "You're not filling me with confidence."

"Wait and see." Tork started to get to his feet. "Now come with me. We might need to go knock on the—"

Just then, out of nowhere, a sharp pain spiked in his side...sharp enough to make him wince and stagger.

"What is it?" asked Rogg. "What's wrong?"

Tork's breath hissed between clenched teeth as he

looked down at his side—but there was no visible sign of an injury there. "Nothing...just a..." He grimaced as the pain spiked again. "Just a cramp."

"Oh, sure." Rogg's voice was full of sarcasm. "And here I was worried something was really wrong with you."

"No need to worry at all." After a moment, the pain finally ebbed, and Tork unclenched...but he secretly worried about the cause of the attack. He worried because in his experience, pain flaring up for no apparent reason signaled something dark indeed. It meant that perhaps, even over a great distance through space, the Blowback link could still transmit physical pain and damage between him and Angar.

In which case, he worried, something bad might have happened to his fellow Horde Lord, wherever he was. If that was true, it might mean Tork was forever stranded on the jungle planet, never to return to his people or the *Hellcyon.*

Which meant he had all the more reason to fight to rid that planet of the scourge of the Caul and their allies.

"I'm fine." He started forward along the weedy edge of the runway, gesturing for Rogg to follow. "Now let's get in a little closer before that door finally opens."

TORK AND ROGG MADE SEVERAL MORE MOVES, GETTING closer every time. Still, the flight center door stayed tightly shut, and no Narl or Caul personnel appeared outside the structure.

The last move brought them within twenty yards of

the building, the perfect spot from which to ambush someone coming out of the place. They waited there for a long time, watching through the rain from the brush—and Tork got wetter and more impatient with each passing moment. The urge to make something happen built in his chest, pushing him to take some kind of action, wise or otherwise.

He was just wondering how many strikes it would take for his battleaxe to chop through the door when a signal went off inside the building—a strident bell ringing continuously. Seconds later, the bell grew even louder as the door finally wrenched free of the ground and slowly rolled upward.

"This is it!" whispered Tork, rising to a crouch and tensing with the axe in his grip. "Follow my lead!"

Before Rogg could say a word, the Horde Lord jumped out of the brush and ran across the paved runway, feet splashing in puddles as he went. The shapeshifter, in his diminutive form, had to work hard to keep up.

Just as the door was high enough to clear Tork's head, he charged inside, axe powered up and ready for action. The first thing he saw was the nose of the golden wedge craft he'd seen enter the hangar the day before, pointing right at him.

The next things he saw were two Narl, one standing on either side of the ship's nose with weapons in hand. Instantly, they swung their rifles up to aim in his direction.

Tork smiled wickedly, made a choice, and veered left.

The Narl on that side got off two shots, sending energy bolts flashing past Tork. Before he could fire a third, Tork cut him in half down the vertical axis. As his spiny blue body split in two, the halves falling in opposite directions, Tork snatched the rifle from his faltering grip and spun to face the other Narl rounding the ship's nose from the right side.

The second Narl pulled the trigger first. Tork deflected his shot with the broad side of his axe's blade, simultaneously firing the rifle he'd seized from his first opponent. Guns weren't his first choice of weapon, but his aim was true; his shot lanced through the Narl's face, blowing it apart like an overripe melon.

It was then that he heard Rogg's shouted warning.

"Behind you! Watch out!"

Time seemed to slow down as Tork whipped around with both weapons at the ready. He saw a creature hovering there, a translucent globular mass glowing with pale gray light, gazing at him with nine filmy yellow eyes arranged in a diamond-shaped grid. Dozens of slimy tentacles dripped from its underside, squirming and slithering in constant motion—but only two of those appendages caught Tork's gaze, curled around pistols that were pointed right at him.

As slow as time seemed to go in that moment, it wasn't enough. Tork thought he moved instantaneously, pulling the rifle trigger and swinging back the axe for a throw... but by then, the beams from the creature's guns were already streaking toward him.

He felt them hit his chest and belly with blistering heat, like hot metal pouring into his body. He pitched over backward, letting go of the axe and rifle at the same time.

As he hit the floor, he heard Rogg cry out...then himself. The bells continued to ring in the flight center.

The last thing he saw before it all went black was the nine-eyed face of the globular creature gliding over him, its tentacles dancing toward him with languid, oozing grace.

PART II
EYE OF THE NEEDLE

CHAPTER 18

HELLCYON

"I don't understand!" said Dr. Mode as she shocked Angar's heart a second time. "He has a mild concussion and a flesh wound to his shoulder. There's no reason he should be going into cardiac arrest!"

Angar's body convulsed, then relaxed. The EKG signal jumped, steadied...then flatlined again.

The team in the med center continued to work feverishly, taking readings and adjusting medications. They surrounded Angar's body on the treatment bed, fighting to keep him alive...the same thing they'd been doing since Quinza Acquiesce had found him near the Skull and called a med team.

Captain Gauge, meanwhile, stood back and watched with grave concern, arms clamped stiffly at his sides. There was much he could have said to urge the team on, but none of it would have mattered. They were all quite well aware of Angar's importance and the need to keep him alive.

"This doesn't make any sense!" snapped Mode. "There's no medical reason we should be losing him!"

Just then, Isabel ran into the room, face flushed and hair mussed. "Losing him?" She elbowed her way to the bed. "Unacceptable!"

"Isabel." Gauge reached for her shoulder.

Shrugging him off, she pulled an oblong silver device from her uniform and held it over Angar's forehead. The device emitted a low hum as she moved it back and forth over him. "Defibrillation won't bring him out of this. He isn't flatlining for medical reasons."

"Then what..."

Isabel adjusted settings on the device, and its hum became a rhythmic warble. "A *technological* issue requires a *technological* solution." Three colored lights on the surface of the device blinked in series—red, blue, gold, red, blue, gold. "Don't you recognize a *blowback* reaction when you see one, Doctor?"

The lights blinked with increasing speed. The warble became a fast-paced, high-pitched trill.

Suddenly, there was a blip on the heart monitor screen. And another.

"Normal sinus rhythm restored," said one of the male medics.

"He's pulling out of it," said a female medic, sounding surprised. "Vital signs stabilizing."

"Of course they are," said Isabel. "I just disengaged the blowback mechanism buried in his brain."

Mode frowned. "What made you realize it was a blowback issue? Its effects have never been proven over such long distances."

"Clue number one," said Isabel as she tweaked the settings on her device. "This guy can still *feel* his partner on the far end of their thinklink—though he's light years away—and thinklinks are only rated effective at a few hundred miles. It's how we're *tracking* him. Does it really surprise us that blowback impacts are coming through loud and clear, too?"

Gauge stepped closer to the table. "Then that might mean...our retrieval mission is now over."

"That's a distinct possibility," said Isabel. "Since the purpose of blowback is to inflict physical effects in one individual that are equal to those experienced by a linked individual..."

"This might mean Tork is dead," said Gauge. "And the blowback almost took Angar with him."

Mode and his assistants took more readings with their instruments, trading their findings in hushed voices over Angar's still form. Now that the fight for his life was over, stress levels in the med center were markedly lower.

"He's stable." Mode nodded at Isabel. "Nice work."

Isabel scowled. "What I want to know is, why the hell was he unconscious on the floor outside the Skull in the first place? Especially when the ship was under attack by the Quinteri."

"Unknown," Gauge said darkly. "According to security feeds, he got in a fight with three humanoids clad entirely in black. We didn't see much, though, because the feeds were intermittent when the ship took heavy fire."

"Assassination attempt?" asked Mode. "Someone angling to become the next Horde Lord?"

"Maybe he wasn't the target," said Isabel. "Maybe he just stumbled upon some threat in progress that had nothing to do with him."

"He can tell us more when he wakes up," said Gauge. "In the meantime, we've got a question to consider. How long do we leave the blowback device switched off?"

Nodding, Mode looked around at his med team. "That's a good question. What if we reactivate it, and he starts dying again?"

"But we can't leave it off forever," said Isabel. "We need to follow the connection to Tork."

"You're right about that," said Gauge. "We've got a course laid in, but it might need correction. We need that link online to get where we're going." He sighed. "Once we finish repairs from the Quinteri attack, which will take some time. *Hellcyon's* lucky to be in one piece after that ambush."

"So are we." Isabel gave him a meaningful look.

"I heard it was a narrow escape," said Mode. "That your team barely got off the *Echelon* in time."

"It was the trip back that almost got us," said Gauge. "Rerox had to do some fancy flying, that's for sure. And Valla and her squadron gave us the fighter escort we needed to reach the hangar deck."

"We nearly lost everything on the first stop of our first mission." Isabel shook her head in disgust. "Over a damn *distress call*, no less. Doesn't bode well for whatever comes next, does it?"

"We need to stay upbeat," said Gauge. "There were

bound to be some bumps along the way, first time out of the barn."

"I'm just saying, this could be a hell of a short quest." With that, Isabel spun and left the med center, leaving Gauge and Mode and the med team to linger there awkwardly around the resting form of the strongest among them.

CHAPTER 19

JUNGLEWORLD

AS THE BEAMS OF ENERGY RIFLES SLASHED THROUGH THE AIR around him, Rogg spun across the hangar of the flight center, barely avoiding them. In his latest attempt at a shapeshift, he'd become a kind of upright propeller covered in bright purple fur, squeezing oily bubbles out of the long, striped tube of his lower body as he flew.

As goofy as he looked, his new form was pretty good at dodging energy bolts fired by the Narl and Cossitora below. There were six of each down there, and they'd been shooting away with abandon for several minutes without success. Rogg just kept swinging out of their paths at the last second, letting the bolts punch holes in the metal ceiling again and again.

Meanwhile, on the floor beside the gold, wedge-shaped ship, Tork's inert body lay momentarily forgotten in a glistening scarlet puddle. From what Rogg could see, he hadn't moved since the Cossitora pilot had blown holes in his chest and belly, cutting short his deadly charge to seize control of the ship.

The only thing that had been moved since Tork's fall was his battleaxe, which one of the Narl had been trying to put to use. It seemed to be too heavy, though, as he couldn't keep it off the floor for long. Every time he tried to raise and swing it, the blade ended up crashing down again, nearly dragging him to the floor with it.

Rogg wasn't having much more success than that, though. As good as he was at dodging energy weapons fire, he couldn't escape the flight center; the Narl had closed the hangar door, trapping him inside. Fighting back wasn't an option, either, as his current form had no offensive capabilities to speak of...and he was worried that if he tried shifting into a form that did, he might end up unable to evade his pursuers.

Gazing down at Tork, he wished the musclebound barbarian had never come his way. If they hadn't met, there would have been no quest to silence the Song, and they wouldn't have ended up meeting tragic ends in the flight center. Rogg's people would have continued to live in misery, but maybe it wouldn't have been as bad as it was now that they'd briefly known hope...and lost it.

Again, a volley of energy bolts flashed toward Rogg, and again he swung away from them. How long would it take for him to wear out and be unable to keep up the dance? He knew he couldn't last forever.

Suddenly, the door to the rest of the complex flew open, and another squad of armed Narl stampeded into the hangar. Roaring with rage, they swung up their rifles and fired away, filling the air with a fusillade of sizzling blasts.

Frantically, Rogg swooped and flipped and spun, trying to evade the burst of firepower...but it was just too much. Bolts slashed everywhere around him, turning the air into a searing storm from which he could not long escape.

Once more, he wished he'd never met Tork, and his gaze slid downward...then stopped. He gasped, unable to believe what he saw below.

Or rather, what he *didn't* see.

The puddle of blood was empty. Either someone had dragged Tork away for nefarious reasons, or...

That was when he heard the first howling scream from one of the Narl reinforcements.

Still dancing between the volleys of energy bolts, Rogg looked in the direction of the scream. His view of the action was blocked by the golden ship...at least until he saw the head of a Narl flying out from behind it.

Multiple Narl stopped shooting at Rogg and charged toward the spot where the head had been launched. Seconds later, more screams erupted from down there, and jets of Narl blood fountained into the air.

Finally, the storm of gunfire that had targeted Rogg died down. Every Narl and Cossitora on the floor scrambled toward the ongoing battle with weapons raised, converging on the force of nature that had claimed the lives of their comrades.

No longer dodging flurries of energy blasts, Rogg was free to go where he wanted. Using the bubbles he ejected to steer himself, he bobbed across the hangar space to see for himself what was happening behind the golden ship.

Weapons fire flashed, and bones shattered. The sound of a mighty blade chopping through flesh filled the air, in counterpoint to the chorus of agonized screams.

Rogg knew who was causing the chaos. It could be only one person. Still, when he circled the ship far enough to see the fighter revealed in full, he felt a shot of disbelief alongside the burst of sheer joy.

Not only was Tork no longer dead, but the gaping wounds in his chest and belly were completely healed. Not only was he back on his feet, but he was swinging his massive battleaxe as if it weighed nothing at all.

Roaring, he split a Cossitora in half diagonally, splattering its slimy guts all over a trio of Narl. Even as the Narl swiped the guts from their eyes, he went through them like a scythe through grain, hacking off one head, then another, then a third.

More Narl and Cossitora died by the blade of his axe, dispatched in a rapid-fire dance of death. Energy bolts kept coming, but every one of them missed—and then he tore apart whoever had fired them.

Like a dervish, he spun through the hostile force, leaving no one intact. Not a single Narl was left standing, not a single Cossitora yet hovered aloft.

And when it was all over, the man who'd seemingly come back from the dead turned his gaze to the shapeshifter hanging overhead. He raised his axe effortlessly, as if he hadn't just swung it dozens of times through dense hides and thick muscle.

And he waved it at Rogg.

"It's safe to come down now," Tork said, grinning. "These bastards won't bother you anymore."

Rogg still drifted near the ceiling, feeling a little shaky from his ordeal. "I thought you were dead!"

"Well, I wasn't!" said Tork. "Lucky for you, huh?"

"But why aren't you?" asked Rogg. "And what happened to the huge *holes* in your chest and stomach?"

"What holes?" Tork looked down at himself and shook his head. "I don't remember ever seeing any."

"Are you some kind of shapeshifter, and you just never told me about it? Have you been a secret shifter all along, Starbarian?"

Tork laughed. "If I was, I'd have put it to use before now, wouldn't I?" With that, he banged the broad side of his axe against the metal skin of the ship with a resounding clang. "Now come give me a hand. The sooner you get down here, the sooner we get this ship in the air and go shut off that damn *Song* that's crippled your people."

CHAPTER 20

HELLCYON

"Don't make me call Security." Dr. Mode wasn't having much luck keeping Angar in bed. "You are *not* cleared for discharge from the med center."

Angar nearly knocked her over in his hurry to get to his feet. Though he'd been conscious for barely five minutes, he had urgent business to attend to. "I feel fine, Doctor."

"You understand that we almost *lost* you, right?" snapped Mode.

" 'Almost,' " said Angar. "And now I'm fine."

Pushing past Mode, he grabbed his sword, which was leaning against the wall. As long as he had a mutiny to stop, he couldn't waste time arguing with Mode about not having permission to leave.

Somehow, he had to figure out who the three black-cloaked mutineers were. He had to do it fast, before they succeeded in seizing command of the *Hellcyon.*

And that wasn't the only thing he had to do fast.

"You're not going anywhere." Mode swooped over and blocked the exit with arms spread wide. "As the ship's chief medical officer, I can override anyone, even the captain...and I'm overriding *you* in this case. Now get back in bed."

"While Tork is dead or dying out there somewhere? Not a chance."

Mode's eyes widened. "You *know* what happened on the other end of the link?"

"I just know there was a feeling of intense pain," said Angar. "Then nothing. *Still* nothing."

"That doesn't mean anything," said Mode. "Your blow-back implant was deactivated, and it still is. He could still be alive."

Angar took a step closer and locked gazes with her. "All the more reason to get moving. The last time I sensed Tork, he was dying or dead. *Anyone* who tries to stop me from saving him will have hell to pay and *then* some."

With that, Angar reached out and dropped a hand on Mode's shoulder. She resisted for a moment, jaw clenched, eyes glinting...then relaxed and stepped aside.

"I'm noting this in my medical log," she told him. "That you disobeyed a direct order to stand down and take additional time to recover from your near-death experience."

Angar smirked. "If you had any idea how many times I've been near death, you wouldn't worry so much."

Then, the door dissolved before him, and he marched out into the corridor. Even as he headed for the Cortex, though, he felt darkness and doubt deep within him—the shadow of death, so stark and familiar.

He also felt the absence of the link to Tork, the silence in place of another living soul connected to his heart and mind. As much as he'd always hated him, he'd grown used to feeling and hearing him on so personal a level. It had kept him reminded of the need to someday kill his worst enemy and take everything for himself.

Even if he had to save him first to make all that possible.

~

"Prepare for launch!"

Those were the first words Angar heard when he entered the Cortex, barked over the noise and chaos by Captain Gauge. The order spurred the crew to work harder and faster as they readied their stations for the ship's next rip.

Angar was glad to see it. Holding position in one star system while Tork was dying or dead in another far away was about the last thing he wanted to do right now.

"Angar." Gauge turned as he approached. "How are you feeling?"

"Fine." Angar was glad Gauge hadn't called him out for leaving the med center early. "Ready for anything."

"Good." Gauge narrowed his eyes and nodded. "I've got a feeling we'll need all hands on deck when we get where we're going. Assuming we know how to get there...?" He raised his voice for the benefit of nearby crew members.

"Course laid in, sir." The holographic display of helm

and navigational instruments flashed and flickered around Lt. Jelani. "No additional recalibrations necessary at this time."

"Well, that's a relief." Gauge nodded at Angar. "We won't have to switch on the Blowback just yet, then."

"Switch it on whenever you want." Angar shrugged. "I'll be fine."

"Will you, though?" Gauge cocked his head to one side. "Why take the chance unless we have no other choice?"

Angar understood. If Tork was indeed dead, and the Blowback system detected that fact, it would make sure Angar ended up the same way.

"I'll be fine." He said it as if he were challenging Gauge to claim otherwise. "Just do whatever you need to do."

"I've got just the thing." Gauge lowered his voice. "I want the mutineers stopped before we reach Caul space."

It was easier said than done, but Angar nodded. Telling Gauge all the reasons he might fail would accomplish nothing. "I'll take care of it."

"I might have a lead for you, actually." Punji's flowery head bobbed down between them on its rubbery stalk. "The ones who attacked you did a *fantastic* job of concealing their identities. They wore head-to-toe camo-suits that blocked all sensors and cameras—even disguised the vibrations of their footfalls and the rhythm of their breathing. They gave the Shipbrain A.I. nothing to calculate their identities with...*almost.*"

"Almost?" said Gauge.

Punji chuckled. "Shipbrain couldn't figure out who they *were*, so it figured out who they *weren't.* It used the process of elimination based on whose whereabouts were detectable during the attack on Angar. We still ended up with more than three suspects, but it's better than 500."

"How many are there, then?" asked Gauge.

"Seventeen," said Punji. "And *surprise!* They aren't all hordespeople."

Angar *was* surprised. "Who are they? Give me the list."

Punji's indigo petals fluttered. "Just sent it to you via thinklink. You might want to start with—"

"I'll start however I choose," snapped Angar as the list appeared before his mind's eye. "And I'll take care of this right away."

"How about a security detail to keep you company?" asked Punji. "You *did* just die in the med center, after all."

Angar leaned toward him, glaring. "I'll pretend you didn't *say* that." Then, he pulled back, spun on his heel, and stormed off, heading for the exit.

He almost felt sorry for the mutineers, given the plans he had in mind for when he found them.

CHAPTER 21

JUNGLEWORLD

FOR ONCE IN HIS LIFE, TORK WISHED HE WASN'T SUCH A thorough slaughterer.

"There's no one alive over here," said Rogg from across the hangar. "Any luck on your side?"

"No." Tork finished rummaging through a pile of severed limbs and heads he'd hacked off in battle, the last place he'd looked for a live specimen. None of the fighters he'd faced was intact, let alone alive enough to fly a manned Caul ship.

Which was a shame, because that had been his only plan for flying the ship from the start. Seize a captive who knew how to pilot, then force him at axe-point to fly the ship to the source of the Song.

But that was no longer an option, thanks to his murderous rampage.

"You couldn't leave one of them alive, could you?" said Rogg, who'd reverted to his rugged obsidian form. "Just one?"

"What can I say?" Tork kicked one of the heads, sending it rolling across the floor. "You'd have been upset too, if they'd killed you."

"Point taken," said Rogg.

The two of them combed the rest of the flight center facility, but the place was deserted. If anyone else had been there, they'd either fled into the jungle or hidden themselves extremely well.

That left Tork and Rogg as the only possible pilots for the ship. Returning to the hangar, they clambered up the fuselage and dropped into the open cockpit, knowing full well they had none of the skills they needed to fly the craft.

Facing the control panel with its multitude of buttons, readouts, switches, and knobs, Tork blew out his breath in frustration. "Maybe I should let you do the driving."

"Me?" Rogg laughed. "At least you've been *inside* a spaceship before!" He gestured over Tork's shoulder at the crowded console of controls before him. "Surely *some* of that must look familiar."

Tork shook his head. "Not even a little." Reaching out, he flipped a switch at random, then turned a knob. Nothing happened.

"Try that red one over there." Rogg pointed. "It looks important."

Tork punched a big red button on the console. He didn't expect anything to happen, and it didn't. The ship remained as still and silent as ever.

"What about that one?" Rogg pointed at a round silver dial with an indentation pressed into it. "It looks like the imprint of a hand, doesn't it?"

Tork nodded. "A three-fingered one."

With that, he leaped out of the ship with axe in hand and down to the floor, where he embarked on a new search. When he returned moments later, he carried the furry blue paw of a Narl, blood oozing from the end where it had been hacked from an enemy arm.

Hopping back into the front seat of the cockpit, Tork pressed the severed paw into the indentation. The paw's three fingers perfectly matched the imprint, and the silver dial glowed with a bright green aura.

Right after that, the entire control console activated at once. Dormant readouts and lights flashed to life, and a black steering wheel assembly emerged from the floor.

"We got it switched on, anyway," said Rogg.

"So what next?" Tork took hold of the steering wheel and turned it back and forth. "This is the only thing I recognize from the ship I was in before."

"I have no clue, Victim Eater." Rogg shook his head. "What were we thinking? We can't fly this thing on our own."

"Don't give up so fast." Tork took a deep breath and let it out slowly. "Help me think this through. How do we get this thing off the ground?"

Suddenly, a gruff male voice spoke in the cockpit. *"Help requested by Narl Sargent Inzar Cawdi Lau, Fifth Battalion Greenmost Occupiers."*

Tork grabbed his axe and shot glances in all directions, thinking an enemy had joined them in the cockpit. Seeing no one, he guessed it must be the ship talking, just as the *Hellcyon* had answered questions when asked.

"*Help provided,*" said the voice. "*Engines activated.*"

The ship shivered, and the cockpit filled with the sound of roaring turbines.

"All we have to do is ask, I guess." Tork shrugged.

"Then what are all the damn *controls* for?" Rogg gestured at the crowded console. "Seems like we could've done without them, doesn't it?"

"Who knows?" Tork raised his voice to be heard clearly over the engine noise by whatever part of the ship was listening. "I want to fly now!" When nothing happened, he thought back and realized he'd used a particular word when the ship's engines had come to life. "*Help* us to fly now!"

As soon as the words left his mouth, the transparent cover slid into place over the cockpit, and the ship lifted off smoothly from the floor. The hangar door rolled up, and the ship drifted toward the opening.

"Wow." Rogg stood on his seat and watched over Tork's shoulder. "We're actually doing this, aren't we?"

Tork smiled. "I *told* you everything was going to work out."

As the ship crossed the threshold, pouring rain hammered on the cockpit like a hail of bullets. The soaking wet jungle fanned out ahead, emerald fronds and vines weighed down by the water's pounding impact.

"*Flight is imminent,*" said the ship. "*Secure all cockpit restraints to avoid injury.*"

"Buckle up!" Rogg dropped back in his seat, pulled a thick strap diagonally across his body, and clicked the metal tongue at the end of the strap into a catch mounted on the side of the seat. He did the same from the other side, the two straps forming a harness in the shape of an X that held him tight against the seat.

Tork did the same, though it took some wrestling to pull the straps over his ultra-muscular body.

"Flight is imminent," said the voice of the ship. *"State your destination."*

Tork lowered his voice and spoke over his shoulder. "What's the place called? The one where they send out the Song?"

Rogg thought for a moment. "Tell it to take us to Gomba Kilo. That puts us in the right direction."

Tork nodded, then addressed the ship. "Our destination is Gomba Kilo. Please help us get there as fast as possible."

"Course laid in," said the ship. *"Launching."*

With that, the golden craft jumped down the runway, its distance from the ground increasing with each passing yard. Just as it reached the runway's end, the ship swooped upward through the torrents of rain, climbing fast as if it faced no resistance at all.

"Hold on!" Rogg grinned as he said it, watching the tops of the jungle trees fall away on either side of the rising craft.

Tork just gazed impassively at the approaching clouds. He hadn't been so close to the sky since he'd leaped through the portal from Io. Now that he was up there, he wished he could just keep going all the way to the stars beyond, then race across the darkness of space until he found his way back to the *Hellcyon*. Only by being trapped on Jungleworld for weeks had he come to appreciate that ship and the good things it had brought him. If he could have snapped his fingers and gotten back to it, he would have done so in a heartbeat.

"I guess flying isn't as hard as we thought it was," said Rogg.

"Yeah," said Tork. "It's easier than I remember."

"At this rate, I'll bet destroying the Song-maker will be easy, too." Rogg chuckled. "I'm kind of looking forward to it."

"If it's anything like coming back from the dead," said Tork, "it won't be much of a challenge at all."

CHAPTER 22

HELLCYON

As the *Hellcyon* hurtled through Rip Space toward Tork's location, Angar charged through the ship's corridors, laser-focused on a different destination.

It had obsessed him since he'd first read the list of possible mutineers provided by Punji. Of the 17 names on that list, one had jumped out at him right away—and that one had pointed to the destination he was about to reach.

The rest of the list was interesting and important, but there could be no other starting point for his investigation. No one else demanded his *immediate* attention.

Still, when he got to the door, he hesitated before entering. His next move had seemed so clear on his way from the Cortex, but now a wave of uncertainty washed over him. If he charged in like a maniac and exploded, he might lose his best chance to identify the other two mutineers who'd attacked him. The more he stayed in control of himself and his emotions, the better he could control the situation.

Taking a deep breath, he reached for the door control...but the door crumbled away before he could trigger it. On the other side, he saw the very person he'd come to see.

His dark-haired firebrand of a wife.

"Well look who's here!" Fists planted on her hips, Vixa sneered up at him. "Quick, let's round up the children and have a party! The great Horde Lord has deigned to bless us with his company!"

"Vixa." Angar gave no sign of his annoyance...or suspicion. "Why aren't you on the hangar deck drilling the crew? We'll be entering Caul space any minute now."

"They're drilling just fine without me." Vixa flapped her hands dismissively. "That crystal guy has it all under control."

"Then where were you going just now, when you opened the door?" asked Angar.

"Coming to find *you*, dear husband." She leaned close, giving him a deeply flirty look.

It was then that he smelled the alcohol on her breath. She wasn't a big drinker, but there it was—and it helped explain her erratic behavior.

What it did *not* explain was why she might be drinking en route to an enemy sector, as the perfect time for launching a mutiny was fast approaching.

"You are *such* an asshole, you know that?" She threw her arms around his neck. "Not *all* of us think you're the next best thing to a god."

Eyes narrowed, he peered at her—and had a sudden thought. What if she *wasn't* the female mutineer he'd fought?

Taking her by the shoulders, he backed her through the doorway. "Where are the others, Vixa? Where are my other wives?"

"I'm the only one you need, my husband." Vixa gave him a long, lusty kiss. "I'm all the wife you'll *ever* need." Her voice was a seductive whisper.

Angar pushed past her and looked around the living quarters they shared with the other wives. As far as he could see, he and Vixa were the only current occupants.

"Where were you during the battle with the Quintero?" he asked her.

"Drilling the crew as you commanded, sir." She made a mocking salute.

"The truth this time." He balled his fists and glared at her. "I won't *ask* you again."

Vixa looked like she had another quip ready, but then she kept it to herself. "I was playing a game, if you must know."

Angar scowled. "What kind of game?"

"Switching places with another wife." She giggled. "I wanted to see what it was like to be someone else...and she *agreed.*"

"Switching places?"

"Wait here." Vixa raised a single index finger and hurried past him to the bedroom. She came back moments later with flowing blonde hair instead of black. "What do you think? Do I look like her or what?"

"Your hair...?" Angar was dumbfounded. "How did you...?"

Vixa gave the long blonde locks a toss. "It's called a wig, Angar. You can have whatever hair you like."

"That's it," said Angar as certain pieces fell into place in his mind. "That's what happened."

"You want to borrow it?" She took off the blonde wig and held it toward him. "I think you'd look just like *Tork* in this."

"You wore this one." Angar pointed at the wig. "Does that mean *Reyel* wore the other?"

"That's how switching places works," said Vixa.

Angar grunted. "So where's the *black* wig, then?"

Vixa shrugged. "If it's not here, she probably has it."

Angar spent the next few minutes searching every inch of the place for the other wig...and coming up empty. It wasn't in the main room, it wasn't in the bedroom, it wasn't anywhere.

When he'd finished, he found Vixa naked on the sofa, wearing the blonde wig. She drained the last of a bottle of clear alcohol and smiled drunkenly at him.

"Horde Lord!" she said. "Let me prove to you that I am worthy of leading the Eastern Horde!"

Angar barely paused on his way out the door. He finally knew he'd been looking for the wrong woman all along. Vixa had never been the mutineer.

Shipbrain had accounted for the whereabouts of a woman with long, blonde hair, not realizing she'd been dark-haired Vixa wearing a wig. The *true* blonde of similar build was the one who'd been out there stirring up trouble with her cohorts.

And giving Angar a surprise beating in the process.

"*Shang* you, then!" hollered Vixa as the door reconstituted behind him. "I'll get power *without* you!"

Angar heard but didn't answer as he ran down the hall. Now that he finally knew who he was looking for, he didn't have a minute to waste.

CHAPTER 23

JUNGLEWORLD

"THIS COULD GET REALLY BAD," SAID ROGG. "I ALREADY FEEL like my head's about to explode."

The shapeshifter sucked in his breath and groaned. The closer the Caul ship flew to the source of the Song at Gomba Kilo, the worse the pain got for him.

"Just let me know if you can't take it anymore," said Tork. "I can drop you off and fly the rest of the way myself."

"Not a chance," snapped Rogg. "I want to *be* there when my people are finally freed."

"You can trust me to finish the mission, you know," said Tork. "I won't let your people down."

"That's not my main reason for staying," said Rogg, "but it's true I'd rather not risk something going wrong when I'm not around to help."

Just then, something hit the ship, sending it spinning along the cloud bank.

"What was *that*?" howled Rogg.

"That strike originated from a ground-based anti-aircraft cannon," explained the ship. *"Additional strikes are imminent from multiple artillery batteries installed in this area."*

Before the ship had finished speaking, another blast sent it tumbling toward the treetops below. Instinctively, Tork grabbed the wheel and pulled; he wasn't sure if the return of control was his doing, but the ship swooped up at the last second and raced for the cloud deck.

"Those are Narl guns," said Rogg. "I guess someone got the word out about this ship being stolen."

"Evasive maneuvers in progress," said the ship.

By now, Tork knew the ship itself was in control, but he kept manhandling the steering wheel in an effort to dodge incoming blasts. One after another, the bright energy beams sizzled past, barely missing as the ship dove, spun, and corkscrewed out of reach.

"We're doing okay," said Rogg. "You're a pretty good pilot, after all."

Tork just grunted and kept swinging the ship away from the blasts. Another one hit, sending the ship fish-tailing into yet another incoming volley.

"I take that back," said Rogg.

As the strikes kept coming, Tork got an idea and raised his voice to address the ship. "Help us climb out of range," he said. "Get us higher than the clouds."

No sooner had he said that, than the ship broke away from the latest barrage and made for greater heights at high speed. The engines whined as it climbed, following a steep angle through the pouring rain into the fluffy gray cloud deck.

Moments later, the ship emerged in the bright blue sky above the clouds. Tork blinked hard as the big red sun blazed in his eyes, making it hard to see.

"I think it worked," said Rogg. "Not a single energy beam up here so far."

"Continue on course at this altitude, ship," said Tork. "Help us reach our destination at Gomba Kilo as fast as possible."

The ship's voice was silent for a moment—then burst over the speakers with sudden urgency. *"Incoming!"*

The ship took another hit and flipped upside-down, knocking Tork's head against the cockpit cover. Engines screaming, it flashed across the sky that way, spinning on its head the way a wheel spins around its hub.

"Flip us right side up!" Tork shouted at the ship. "And by the way, what just *hit* us? Aren't we out of range of the artillery batteries?"

"Latest airstrike was inflicted by a robot drone," said the ship. *"A second strike is imminent."*

True to its word, another hit rocked the ship. As it bounced across the sky, Tork got a look at the attacking drone—a small gun platform powered by a central propeller and a smaller one on the elbow of each of four bent arms. Black gun barrels hung around the body, all pointed in the golden ship's direction.

As Tork watched, energy bolts lanced from two of those barrels, stabbing toward the ship.

"Brace for impact," said the ship, just before it rocked violently.

"I see another one coming!" shouted Rogg. "And another after that!"

The latest two drones closed in, blasting away as they flew. The golden ship was about to be boxed in and blown to pieces.

"Ship! Destroy the drones!" Tork barked the commands though he had no idea if the ship was equipped with weapons.

It was.

A sudden flurry of energy bolts poured out from under the ship and blew the drones to smithereens. Within seconds, all that remained of the attackers were three clouds of smoke, debris, and flame.

"Wow!" said Rogg. "I didn't *know* we were packing *that* much firepower!"

"*Now* we've got a fighting chance." Tork grinned. "We might just make it to Gomba Kilo after all."

"Oh, great." Rogg winced. "My head is *already* killing me."

CHAPTER 24

HELLCYON

R EYEL WAS GONE LIKE A GHOST. T HE *HELLCYON'S* surveillance systems couldn't find her anywhere. Search teams sent out by Major Schist had exactly the same lack of success.

That was all the more reason for Angar to personally search every corner of the ship himself. Since Reyel was his wife, he felt responsible for bringing her in before she did any damage...and he wanted badly to pay her back for betraying him. He'd insisted on bringing her aboard because she was family; turning against him and taking action without his knowledge or permission was inexcusable.

Head swimming with thoughts of what he was going to do with her, he charged through the ship with crackling sword in hand. He barged into every office and department, overturned every crew member's quarters, and smashed up plenty of furniture along the way. He questioned everyone he met with fierce intensity, even threatened some with grave bodily harm if they looked the wrong way or said the wrong thing.

And yet, she continued to elude him. Her absence was so complete, he started to wonder if somehow she *had* left the ship.

As he got to the last few places he hadn't searched, he was giving up hope. However she'd managed to hide from him, his door-to-door search was not enough to find her.

It was then, in the forward section near the Skull, that he came across Quinza. She glided around a corner, butterflies whirling around her head, and he instantly felt calmer and better about everything.

"Hello, Angar," she said. "It's good to see you."

"Good to see you, too." He smiled. "I don't suppose you've seen my wife, Reyel, lately?"

Quinza's butterflies fluttered as she shook her head. "Why are you looking for her? Is she all right?"

"She's part of a mutiny," he said. "And we can't find her anywhere. She's just disappeared."

Quinza looked deeply sad. "I'm so sorry to hear that, Angar. I can't imagine how you must feel right now."

Angar nodded. "I've had better days."

"It could have been worse," said Quinza. "At least you didn't die in the med center."

"No thanks to Reyel," said Angar. "I wouldn't have been *in* the med center if not for her."

"That's terrible, Angar." Reaching up, Quinza lightly touched his cheek with her warm, soft fingers. "Sometimes, this is how it works for people like us. Those with the greatest gifts are afflicted with the greatest disappointments."

"Speaking of gifts, do you have any way to find her?" asked Angar. "Could you feel her presence, even if she's masking it somehow?"

Quinza shook her head. "I'm sorry, but I'm not a tracker. What about you?"

He frowned. "I said, I've been looking everywhere and haven't found her."

"I meant what if you could feel her presence. What if that's another power you have, like breathing without air on Io?"

"If I'm a tracker, I'm not very good at it," said Angar. "She *has* to be somewhere on this ship, but I sure can't tell you where."

"Gods don't always know everything they can do right away," said Quinza. "Sometimes, their powers can lie dormant for decades while they live out normal mortal lives."

"I keep telling you, I'm no god. I can't..."

"At least try," said Quinza. "Close your eyes and reach out with your mind."

If it had been anyone else asking, Angar would never have done it. Closing his eyes, he stood there in the corridor and tried to concentrate on finding Reyel—reaching out with his mind in a way he'd never tried before. He pictured different parts of the ship and imagined Reyel in them, her distinctive features and form and voice and scent mingling with the walls and floor and contents of the rooms. He tried to feel for her, to pick out where his sense of her was strongest...and he came up empty.

"Nothing." He opened his eyes. "Like I told you, I'm no god."

"At least tell me the place you thought of most often just now," she said. "What place came through most clearly?"

He thought about it. "The Skull." He shrugged. "But that's my favorite place aboard the ship."

"Come with me." Gesturing for him to follow, she headed back up the corridor the way she'd come.

A few turns later, they approached the door to the Skull. A few of her butterflies flew ahead of them and landed on its flat, gray surface, beckoning them with gently fanning wings.

Reflexively, Angar stepped ahead of her, though he didn't expect to find any kind of danger inside. He waved his hand at the glass disk on the wall beside the door, the way he'd done so many times before.

But nothing happened. The door didn't dissolve, scattering the butterflies, and admit him to the room.

He tried again, passing his hand over the disk, and got the same result. The door remained resolutely in place.

"What the *shang?*" He tried two more times, then pulled his sword from the scabbard.

"Wait!" Quinza caught his arm before he could swing back the weapon, meanwhile tapping her earlobe to activate her com link. "Shipbrain, open the door to the Skull."

"The door mechanism is broken," said the Shipbrain. *"An engineer must repair it manually. Recommend you contact..."*

She cut off the computerized voice, tapping her

earlobe to make another call. "Engineering? We have a faulty door mechanism on deck..."

Before she could finish, Angar's sword flashed over his shoulder and crashed into the top edge of the door, biting deep in the intractable metal.

"Never mind, Engineering." Quinza sighed and cut the call. Her butterflies abandoned the door and returned to their roosts on her head.

Teeth clenched, Angar dragged the blade of the sword downward, cutting a slit in the substance of the door. He stopped at the bottom, wrenched the blade free, and stabbed it into the middle of the cut he'd made.

Then, with the blade wedged deep, he put all his strength into forcing it to one side. Grunting with effort, he worked to pry open the split section of the door as Quinza watched.

Slowly, the metal peeled back, widening the opening enough for him to push the blade through further and give him more leverage. His grunts got louder as he dug in and pried harder—then went from grunts to roars as his struggle increased.

The metal fought him every step of the way...and then he overcame it. The section he'd been prying finally peeled the rest of the way, rolling aside to reveal the opening he'd made.

Without hesitation, then, he squeezed through the gap. It was a tight fit, but he made it through into the chamber of the Skull.

As he cleared the opening and put both feet down on the other side, his gaze scanned the room...and stopped. What he saw...

"In Yorg's name..." His voice was hushed as he called upon his god.

"What is it, Angar?" Quinza asked from the corridor. "What do you see?"

He needed to cross the room, but he couldn't make his feet move. What was over there, sprawled on the floor beneath the ruby eyes of the *Hellcyon*, was something he hadn't expected...something he hadn't wanted, no matter how angry he'd been with her.

The body lay absolutely still, limbs splayed at unnatural angles. Glistening blood pooled under it, the same blood soaking the clothes...

The same blood that had turned the long blonde hair bright crimson.

It was her. She had been in the Skull after all, the last place he had looked.

And she was, indeed, gone like a ghost.

"I don't understand," he said, feeling numb and in pain at the same time. "If Reyel is dead, then who is the mutineer?"

As he said it, another question came to mind, a question with deadly implications of its own.

If Reyel is dead, who killed her?

CHAPTER 25

JUNGLEWORLD

JUDGING FROM ROGG'S REACTION, THE GOLDEN SHIP WAS almost on top of the Song source at Gomba Kilo. The shapeshifter was screaming his lungs out, beating the back of Tork's seat with his obsidian fists and feet. The pain brought on by the Song as it played in his brain was so excruciating, he flew into periodic seizures, his whole body thrashing with uncontrollable convulsions until they mercilessly, temporarily, stopped.

Tork knew that dropping him off before they reached the target would be for the best, but Rogg was determined to stay aboard no matter what. Though Tork was sure he could get him out if he tried, he also thought it might do more damage than flying the rest of the way with him...to Rogg, especially.

So the two of them kept flying forward above the cloud deck, Rogg howling in agony, Tork holding on to the wheel as the ship dodged and battled squadrons of armed drones. The drones surged up from below with guns blazing, attacking with fierce precision—only to be blasted to bits before they could do any major damage. They were like angry hornets, swarming in greater numbers the closer the ship got to Gomba Kilo.

Then, suddenly, they were gone. Just as Rogg's screams grew louder than ever, the drones stopped coming, leaving nothing but empty cloud deck ahead.

But the peace was not to last.

"Please tell me we're about to blow the thing up." Rogg stopped screaming but was still panting from the pain. "Tell me it's almost over."

Just then, the ship's nose dipped, and the craft dove into the clouds. When it emerged under the deck, a different view opened up before them—a vast plain cleared of jungle, dominated by a massive metal dish sunk into the ground. A towering spindle rose from its center, braced by taught cables all around, an antenna so tall it seemed like it might scrape the base of the cloud deck.

Even with his minimal understanding of science, Tork thought it looked exactly like something that could broadcast a powerful signal around a planet.

"It's almost over," he said. "Hang on just a little longer."

As he said those words, however, a powerful blast exploded against the ship, throwing it spinning off course.

The ship quickly adjusted, stopping the spin and whipping around to face whatever had fired upon it. It was then that Tork saw what they were up against, and his blood ran cold.

A huge ship hung there, many times larger than Tork and Rogg's golden one. It was an enormous crystalline warship, a destroyer studded with cannons from top to bottom and edge to edge of its gargantuan wingspan.

And every one of its guns was pointing at the little golden ship.

"Looks like we've run into a slight roadblock," said Tork. "Hold on, this could get a little bumpy."

"You mean it wasn't bumpy *before?*" Rogg groaned long and loud.

"Help us!" shouted Tork, raising his voice to the volume the ship responded best to. "Get us past that big ship out there! Then take us to the giant spire in the middle of that bowl!"

"The transmitter dish, you mean?"

"Yes," said Tork, though he didn't really know what a transmitter dish was. Adrenaline burned through his bloodstream as he kept his eyes fixed on the crystal behemoth. At any second, he knew, its mighty array of guns could start blasting. If the golden ship were still hovering in one place when that happened, it would be the end of the line for him and Rogg.

"Prepare for extreme evasive maneuvers," said the ship. *"You may experience some physical discomfort in the immediate future."*

Rogg's agonized cries were louder than ever. The way he battered the back of Tork's seat left no doubt in Tork's mind that the transmitter dish was the source of the Song.

The ship shivered as its engines built up power, getting ready to move. Across the plain, Tork saw red lights dance in the depths of the enemy's guns, getting ready to fire.

"We're ready!" snapped Tork. "Let's go!"

Still, the ship sat and vibrated, the whine of its engines rising. The red light in the enemy's guns grew stronger, flowing along the length of the barrels.

"I said *let's go!*" shouted Tork. "Whoever they are, they..."

Before he could finish his sentence, the ship took off, heading straight for the crystal behemoth. Tork thought they might collide, and he held his breath...but the golden ship veered away at the last possible second, just as the behemoth's big guns blazed to life.

A barrage of energy beams slashed through the air, instantly evaporating swaths of rain as they flashed through it. Every shot missed the golden ship, which had swooped away before the assault and arrowed in the direction of the transmitter.

They wouldn't keep missing for long, though. The behemoth may have been huge, but it wasn't slow at all. No sooner had the golden ship darted away, than the crystalline giant leaped after it, unleashing a fresh fusillade at its tail.

The golden ship's head start shrank fast. The bolts of enemy fire were everywhere, carving past in a blinding, sizzling display. If the golden ship had been only slightly less agile, it would have been hacked to bits in seconds.

As it was, the ship danced between blasts like a hummingbird, dodging one after another with a breathtaking series of rolls and swerves and dives. It couldn't escape forever, as the behemoth was catching up, but it didn't have to—just long enough to reach the transmitter dish.

Rogg screamed like he was out of his mind, and Tork ignored it. Other aspects of the crisis demanded his attention.

"Ship, prepare to fire all weapons at the tower in the middle of the transmitter," he said.

"Antenna!" Rogg shouted unexpectedly. "It's called an antenna!" Then he went back to screaming as the torture continued.

"Prepare to destroy the antenna!" Tork barked.

"Preparing," said the ship.

One of the energy bolts finally hit, then, rocking the golden ship hard and pitching it into a spin. That threw it into the path of another bolt, and another, that hacked off bits of the ship.

"Fuselage compromised," said the ship. *"Flight control damaged. Rerouting systems."*

The ship corrected its spin and flung itself back on course to the transmitter—but the ride wasn't as smooth as before. Tork was sure it wasn't as fast as before, either. The behemoth glided up, guns flashing, and loomed over the golden ship like a great beast dwarfing the morsel it intends to devour.

"Faster!" shouted Tork. "They're right on top of us!"

"Given current damage and fuel level, one booster firing is possible," said the ship. *"But further airborne activity will cease after that."*

"What about weapons?" asked Tork. "Will they still fire when we get there?"

"If current state continues," said the ship. *"And catastrophic damage is not inflicted."*

Tork didn't even have to think about it. "Then go!" If he had only one chance, he had to take it. "Fire the booster!"

The ship followed his order. The engines roared with a surge of power, then cut it loose in a single burst of speed.

The crystalline ship was left behind, firing volleys of energy bolts in the golden ship's wake. One, then another grazed the golden ship, but the damage done wasn't enough to end the booster-propelled flight.

The transmitter antenna raced closer. Its proximity made Rogg go berserk in the back seat, shrieking and pounding on the sides of the cockpit.

"Prepare to fire all weapons at the antenna," commanded Tork.

"Preparing," said the ship. *"All weapons are fully charged and locked on target."*

Tork wanted to make sure his guns fired at close range, maximizing their accuracy and impact. Heart pounding, he waited as the antenna zoomed closer, enlarging with each passing second.

Just as he was about to give the order to fire, one of the behemoth's guns tagged the golden ship, making it lurch downward at a sharp angle. He thought the ship might crash—but it somehow pulled out of the stall and pushed on toward the antenna. The jolt from the booster was gone, though, so there wasn't much forward momentum left.

There wasn't much *time* left, either. *"Airborne activity*

will cease in thirty seconds," said the ship. *"Prepare for unpowered descent."*

"Fire all weapons at the antenna!" shouted Tork. "Now!"

Every gun aboard the golden ship fired at once. The ship's aim was perfect; every energy bolt hit the same spot on the antenna and held, focusing all the raw destructive power at the ship's command on the one slender spike towering over the vast white plain.

Even in the midst of a tropical downpour, the target point quickly became superheated. The metal blazed yellow, then bright cherry red—and the power kept coming.

"Airborne activity will cease in ten seconds," said the ship. *"Prepare for imminent unpowered descent."*

"Come on, come on," said Tork. "Hurry up."

The metal softened and bent—slowly at first, then faster. The once rigid antenna folded over at the heated midpoint, swinging downward...then broke at the bend, snapping in two.

Suddenly, Rogg stopped screaming and thrashing. "It stopped. It finally...stopped..."

Tork had time for only the quickest smile before the golden ship started to sink.

"Brace for impact!" said the ship. *"Brace for impact!"*

Tork gripped the sides of the cockpit and held his breath. The golden ship slipped, then fell like a stone, leaving the remains of the antenna to be pounded by incoming fire from the fast-approaching crystalline ship.

Gritting his teeth, Tork watched as the ground raced toward him. It was too late to do anything but fall—

comforting himself, as he went, that at least his death had accomplished something meaningful.

It made him proud to think that even there on Jungle-world, so far from the home he'd always known, he had managed to secure a spectacular victory against incredible odds.

CHAPTER 26

HELLCYON

"I'M SORRY FOR YOUR LOSS," SAID CAPTAIN GAUGE. "I'M SO, so sorry."

Angar just glared at Reyel's bloody corpse, watching as a medical team clad in white plastic hazmat suits examined her remains. He felt dazed at the sight of his wife, the mother of two of his children, reduced to a still and silent ruin on the floor of the Skull.

"I thought she was one of the mutineers," he said. "I was *sure* of it."

"Maybe she was." Punji loped by, holding a silver scanner board studded with colorful buttons. "We don't know the whole story yet. Maybe she was a mutineer, and her comrades turned on her."

"Maybe she changed her mind and tried to stop them," said Gauge. "Maybe she was a hero in the end."

Angar would have preferred her to be alive, instead. "I *will* get to the truth of this." His voice was a growl. "If I have to *tear* this ship apart to *do* it."

"Please wait." Gauge reached out and put a hand on Angar's shoulder. "We are *deep* in Caul space, and we *need* this ship to rescue Tork. The fate of the galaxy *literally* depends on it."

Angar shook off Gauge's hand. He stood there and seethed, his fists clenched so tight they looked like they might blow apart at any moment.

"Unfortunately," said Punji, "the security camera network on this deck was deactivated by a virus during the hour preceding her murder. We've got zero recorded evidence of the killing or what came before or after it."

"So track the virus," said Gauge. "How did it gain access to the system? Who put it there?"

"Working on it," said Punji.

"For that matter, will it jeopardize our mission?" asked Gauge. "Seems like a big coincidence, this all happening just as we're about to face Caul forces."

"My thoughts exactly." Punji's white-mottled indigo petals fluttered as he nodded. "Though that implies something we've haven't considered, doesn't it?"

Angar scowled at his dead wife, his thoughts roiling with hatred and rage. "Infiltration," he said darkly. "By agents of the Caul."

Gauge sighed. "We took precautions, but they may not have been enough."

"My people said much the same thing," said Punji, "just before the Caul wiped them out of existence."

The three of them fell silent for a while after that.

Then, Dr. Mode rose from beside the body and cleared her throat inside the baggy hazmat suit. "I have a cause of death for you," she said, "and it's not as obvious as you might think."

"Tell us," said Gauge.

"The damage you see? The bloody knife wounds?" Mode gestured at the body behind her. "They were inflicted post-mortem." Angar frowned. "After death," she added for his benefit. "Reyel was already dead from another cause when she was slashed up like that."

"What other cause?" asked Gauge.

"Poisoning," Mode said grimly. "Reyel died from a potent poison I can't identify...and her death, I'm sorry to report, was *far* from painless."

"CAPTAIN GAUGE, REPORT TO THE CORTEX." CULMA Doreen's voice was urgent over the shipwide 'com. *"Captain Gauge, report to the Cortex."*

Gauge responded with no less urgency, sprinting through the ship with Angar close behind. The Cortex door fell away before him, and he and Angar charged through without slowing.

"Report," snapped Gauge, looking at the big screen on his way to the center seat. "What planet is that, and why is it surrounded by ships?"

"That planet is our destination." Isabel, at her science station, flashed a look across the Cortex at Angar. "According to our Horde Lord's directions."

"Tork's down there, then?" Gauge turned to Angar. "How's the signal?"

Angar felt for the blowback link, probing its strength. With everything that had happened lately, he hadn't paid any attention to it in a while—but now that he focused on it, he did notice a change.

"It's stronger." Gazing at the huge green orb on the screen, he felt Tork's presence coming through the link loud and clear. He also felt waves of pain and confusion emanating from the other end of the connection, though he didn't mention that part. "I sense him down there, all right."

"Excellent," said Gauge. "Now can somebody please tell me what all those *ships* are doing out there?"

"They were there when we dropped out of Rip Space," Rerox Demagorn said from the tactical station. "One hundred ships from a range of Caul subject species, plus a bunch we don't even recognize. Intentions unknown, though their guns are all pointing at the planet...so far."

"No contact yet?" asked Gauge.

"None," said Doreen, "but we haven't been here long."

"They must have noticed the Rip," said Isabel.

"Unless they were distracted," said Demagorn. "They've got a lot of *firepower* aimed at that planet."

"The same planet Tork is on." Gauge glanced over his shoulder at Angar. "Coincidence?"

Though his frame of mind was grim, Angar managed a smirk. "No chance."

Gauge grinned and nodded. "Then I guess we better take him off their hands before someone gets hurt."

"The *Caul*, that is." Demagorn's gravelly laugh sounded like rocks banging around in a metal box.

Gauge got up and walked to the screen, staring at the armada surrounding the planet. "Easy-peasy, right? All we need to do is get past the fleet out there, find and extract our man from the planet's surface, and Rip out of here before we're blown to smithereens."

"Sounds almost *too* easy, doesn't it?" said Isabel.

"Give me options, people," said Gauge. "Preferably, options that don't get us blown up."

"We go in with guns blazing," said Demagorn. "They've never come face to face with the *Hellcyon* before. We'll smash right through them and get what we came for!"

"That's one option," said Gauge. "Next?"

"Tell them we're a Caul vessel," said Isabel. "Pull in close and slip a shuttle to the surface when no one's looking."

Gauge nodded. "Anyone else?"

"Diversions." Angar stepped forward and pointed with the tip of his sword at the planet on the screen. "We send out squads of fighters to occupy their attention. The *Hellcyon*, too. Meanwhile, the real rescue shuttle slips past them and brings him back." He traced a path to the planet's surface with his sword, then traced a path back up into orbit. "I bring back Tork."

"Winner, winner, chicken dinner." Gauge smiled. "Now *that's* a plan I might *bet* on, if I were a betting man."

"I'm glad you like it." Angar sheathed his sword and headed for the door. "I'll get suited up right now for the flight."

"You're planning to go to the surface?" asked Gauge.

"Of course I am," said Angar. "It was my idea."

"We can't put *both* of you at risk," said Gauge. "Especially not in a battlefield setting."

"Yes we can," Angar said over his shoulder. "It's not like I'd trust anyone *else* to go get him."

"You can't go!" snapped Gauge. "You'll stay *here* on the *Hellcyon*."

Angar stopped and turned, casting an ominous glare at the captain. "Is that a direct order?"

For a moment, the Cortex was silent except for the beeps and buzzes and whistles of the instrumentation—holographic and otherwise—in action. All the crew members watched and waited, wondering what the outcome of the test of wills would be. Who would be the first to blink?

In the end, it was Gauge. "All right." He couldn't have stopped Angar if he'd wanted to, and he'd known it. "We'll send you down...but it won't be in a shuttle."

"Then what *will* we fly that has room for more than two people?"

"You'll see," said Gauge.

"Fine," said Angar. "As long as Schist is my pilot."

"You'll get who I give you," Gauge said firmly. "Now *go*. What the hell are you still doing loitering around my command center?"

Angar turned and left the Cortex without another word. He'd won the battle of wills...so why did he feel like he'd lost somehow?

"All right, people!" Gauge shouted behind him. "Show's over! Arm all weapons, power up the shields, and scramble fighters! Go-time is in t-minus fifteen minutes!"

PART III
BATTLE ROYALE

CHAPTER 27

JUNGLEWORLD

"TORK? STARBARIAN? CAN YOU HEAR ME?"

The voice seemed to come from a million miles away, whispering in the all-consuming darkness. It was the only thing Tork was aware of except for the darkness, the absolute blackness that welled within him.

"There's no pulse," said the distant voice. *"I know you must be dead, but...you were dead once before, weren't you? You were dead and came back.*

"It's what you do."

Tork was so far gone, he barely registered the words. His mind had faded almost to nothing as he floated in the darkness. Everything that could have been considered Tork Gallgore was drifting away on the bobbing tide, all the bits and pieces moving farther and farther apart.

All but the uncomprehending awareness of that faraway voice.

"Please, Tork. You have to see this. You have to see what you've done for my people."

Just then, a tiny flame sparked to life in the shadows, a flickering focus of warmth and light. The pieces of Tork that had been drifting apart reversed course and began drifting toward it.

Slowly, the bits of him came together again, coalescing in the blackness. The flame at the heart of him grew stronger and brighter, in turn attracting more of his scattered substance to unite.

"I knew it!" said the voice, which wasn't quite so distant anymore. *"Your heart's beating! I knew you'd come back to us!"*

Something kicked within him then, and the flame became a roaring fire. The darkness parted all around it, dispelled by the blaze of his rekindled existence.

Suddenly, he knew who he was, and all his senses reconnected with his body and mind. He remembered where he was, and what had happened—the golden ship falling, the antenna collapsing. He had fallen so hard, it had shattered him, cast him into a vast darkness of unknowing.

And now, he was back, and his eyes were fluttering open. The rain had stopped. Rogg, in his craggy, obsidian form, was staring down at him with a glowing ruby gaze.

"Welcome back!" said Rogg. "I *knew* you'd come back to us!"

Tork slowly opened his mouth. "Wh-what..." It felt strange, trying to operate the parts of his physical self again. "What...do you mean...*us?*"

"My people, of course! The ones you saved!" Rogg gestured, and multiple figures moved into view.

Tork recognized them from the village he'd helped liberate earlier—amorphous, green-skinned beings with big, bright eyes. They swayed and rippled like sheets in a breeze, making soft humming sounds as they gazed down at him.

"They came to thank you," said Rogg. "For the first time in a long time, the Song is finally silent! They—we— are finally free!"

As he said it, the Gossa changed shape, each one becoming something different. One became a spiny blue Narl, another a jellyfish-like Cossitora. One turned into an ebony dragon, another a giant scorpiopede. One even ended up looking exactly like Tork, complete with long blond hair and beard.

As Tork watched, they traded forms, each one transforming to match the appearance of another. They did it slowly at first, then with increasing speed, until each being held its shape for no longer than a heartbeat.

Then, they all settled on Tork's shape and held it. Smiling down at him, they all spoke at once in his voice.

"Thank you," they said. "Thank you for restoring the gifts we were born with."

"Happy to help." With a wince, Tork pushed himself up to a seated position. He'd come back to life, but not without damage. "It's never good when someone takes away the thing that gives you power."

"It will never happen again," said one of the Torks. "No one will *ever* put the Song in our heads again."

"We will root out and execute every last one of them," said another of the Torks. "Every invader in the world."

"But not you, of course," Rogg told the real Tork with a smile. "You never have to worry."

Just as he said it, Tork heard approaching shouts and the whine of weapons fire. Energy beams slashed through the air, striking three of the Tork copies—and splashing off harmlessly as the Gossa changed their bodies to reflective silver metal at the last instant.

Looking in the direction the shots were fired from, he saw a team of twelve Narl marching forward through the wreckage of the antenna in the heart of the vast metal transmitter dish. They blasted shot after shot from their massive rifles, never slowing their implacable advance.

"Surrender!" shouted the one in front, his booming voice amplified by some kind of throat mic system that was part of his armor. "Surrender or die!"

The Gossa never said a word. As Tork struggled to his feet and tried to shake off the lingering daze from his resurrection, they changed shape in unison, becoming a pack of monstrous purple beasts with faces that were little more than gaping maws studded with fangs. Shrieking, they charged as one, hurtling their scaly, muscular bodies like reptilian buffalo at the enemy.

The bolts from the Narl's guns tagged them again and again but had no effect. The Gossa kept charging as if the weapons were nonexistent, then slammed into the Narl with concussive force. They tore them apart like cats ripping apart mice, tossing bits of them in the air with gleeful savagery.

Tork stopped trying to join the fight and just stood

there with Rogg, taking it in. He'd always considered the barbarians of the Hordes to be the greatest fighters anywhere, but the Gossa cast his assumptions in a new light. He had never seen warriors move with speed, ferocity, and power, chewing through a dozen heavily armed and armored soldiers like a buzzsaw.

They were done in seconds, leaving the ground soaked with blood and littered with mangled body parts. Throwing back their fang-studded faces, they howled in triumph, sending their own terrible Song echoing in the distance.

Just as they turned and loped back from their gruesome victory, Tork finally spotted his battleaxe amid the wreckage of the golden ship, some thirty feet away. He resisted the instinctive urge to run and grab it before the Gossa arrived.

When they got closer, they changed shape, again taking on Tork's form. Blond hair streaming in the breeze, they strode toward him with grave smiles on what should have been his visage alone.

"What do you think?" said one of the Gossa Torks.

"Impressive," said the actual Tork.

"They got what they deserved," said Rogg. "After the suffering they put us through."

"Their suffering has only begun," said another of the Torks.

"We will finish what we started long ago," said another. "What they chained our mind and power to prevent. we will execute *every last one of them.*"

"Every single invader will die," said one of the other Torks. "Every one of them *everywhere.*"

"Every one of them on *this* planet," said another Tork, "and *beyond.*"

"Our crusade begins *today*," said another Tork. "We are *all* united on this. Especially Rogg, who found the means to *free* us so our campaign of vengeance can begin again!"

With that, the group of Torks all stared at Rogg, waiting for his response. Rogg, flustered, shuffled his blocky obsidian feet and bobbed his head nervously.

Then, he also took the form of Tork. "Kill them all!" He shook his beefy fist in the air. "The Caul and every last one of their despicable servants!"

"And their families!" chimed in one of the Torks. "And their families' families!"

"Yes!" agreed Rogg with another shake of his fist. "And their despicable families, too!"

"Never shall a descendant of their blighted species darken the universe again!" said a Tork. "Just as we have punished *countless* species before, so will we punish *these* abominations!"

They all cheered with special enthusiasm at that, including Rogg...though Tork thought he noticed a flicker of something in Rogg's eye that could have been caused by something other than overwhelming, bloodthirsty vengefulness.

CHAPTER 28

HELLCYON

"BATTLE STATIONS!" THE CALL WENT OUT OVER THE COM system, echoing through the ship. *"All personnel, report to battle stations!"*

Angar did not need a spacesuit, but he put one on anyway, just like all the other pilots and crew getting ready for launch on the hangar deck.

The silver-skinned suit was uncomfortable, though it had been specially made for his muscular form—but he knew he had to wear it. He didn't understand why he could breathe in a vacuum, and he didn't want anyone to know he could do it except Quinza...so on went the suit.

And then it was T-minus one minute until go-time.

Looking around as suited-up pilots and crew charged toward the fighters lined up along the hangar doorway into space, he stood there with his helmet under his arm and had no idea where to go. No one had told him what ship he'd be boarding or who his pilot would be.

Just as he was thinking about tossing someone out of a fighter and commandeering it for himself, someone jabbed him hard in the shoulder. Whirling, he expected some kind of confrontation with an overzealous flight deck supervisor, maybe ending in a scrap if he was lucky.

Instead, he saw the blue-glowing head of a crystalline man grinning back at him.

"Schist!" So it turned out Gauge had given him his favorite pilot after all.

"Fair warning, Horde Lorde." Schist handed him a small brown paper bag. "You might need this."

Angar frowned and took the bag. "For what?"

"Getting sick." Schist nodded. "It's going to take some extra-fancy flying to get past all those ships out there."

"Ha!" Angar threw the bag at him, and he caught it. "Do your worst, diamond head. I can take it."

"Don't say I didn't warn you." Schist stuffed the bag in a pocket of his spacesuit. "So how's the Tork signal? Coming in loud and clear?"

"Better than it has since Io. Don't worry, I'll lead us straight to that son of a bitch...assuming we have some kind of *ship*, that is."

Schist chuckled. "Oh, we've got a ship." His crystalline form changed colors from calming blue to the white of excitement as he pointed across the deck behind Angar.

Gasping in surprise was something Angar just never did...but he did it *this* time. At the far end of the flight deck, a familiar vessel was rolling out of one of the maintenance bays, five times the size of any of the fighters currently lined up and preparing to launch.

"The dragon?" Angar's expression shifted from surprise to pure, fierce joy. *"The dragon?"*

"Hell yes," said Schist. "Now aren't you glad you didn't punch somebody's lights out and steal one of those piddly-ass fighter planes instead?"

The ship had a lizard-like body with a long neck, giant wings, and a tail barbed with man-sized spikes. It was covered in gleaming black scales from nose to tail, and its legs ended in feet tipped with jagged claws.

It looked like a dragon right down to the reddish glow from its nostrils and the smoke curling from its fire-breathing mouth. Angar remembered how it had felt to see the thing coming back on Earth, how his heart had beat faster as it had attacked him and Tork. He had thought it *was* a dragon back then and had fought for his life accordingly, only to have the thing defeat him and Tork together and scoop them up for the trip to the *Hellcyon.*

Now, it was *his* ship—for this mission, at least—and he would use it against the odds to rescue Tork.

As Schist led him across the deck to the dragon ship, fighters leaped through the hangar doorway into space, launching one after another. By the time Angar got to the dragon ship, the entire line was gone, slashing through the starry darkness toward the hardship to come.

Schist rapped on the dragon ship's side, and a section of gleaming black hide opened toward him. As the door came to rest on the hangar deck floor, Schist hurried up the steps inside it, disappearing into the vessel.

With his sword in one hand and his helmet in the other, Angar followed.

Though he'd been inside the ship before, he didn't remember the experience. As an unconscious captive, he hadn't realized the interior was gleaming black like the outside of the craft, with numerous touches that reflected the dragon's personality. He hadn't seen that the two pilot couches had dragon heads and wings built into the headrests. He hadn't noticed that the screens on the wall in front of them were framed by dragonlike spines, and numerous controls on the pilots' console were shaped like claws.

This time, however, he noticed...and *loved* it. Now *this* was a warship with the spirit of a great and savage beast built into its bones, its fabric.

It was the kind of ship a Horde Lord might have built, if he'd had the technology.

Schist threw himself into the pilot's couch on the right and instantly started playing the controls. "So what do you think?"

Angar ran his hand over the jagged edge of the console and shrugged. "It's all right."

"She's the best we've got, aside from the *Hellcyon*." Schist gestured for Angar to sit beside him. "Flies like a dream and fights like a bastard."

Angar frowned as he sat. "Does the fire-breathing work in space? There's no air out here, right?"

"The fire only works in a planetary atmosphere, you're right," said Schist. "But who needs a flamethrower when you've got energy guns, particle beams, missiles, and an animate superstructure capable of significant destructive interventions?"

"What's an animate super...super...?"

Schist flicked a set of switches in rapid succession. "The dragon can tear apart ships with its claws and tail. I'm telling you, this thing's a *monster.*"

"I hope so." Angar didn't show he was impressed. "We're going to *need* one to get through this and bring back Tork."

"Believe me, this is the ship you want for a mission like this," said Schist. "She will get the job done."

With that, he punched a button on the console, and multicolored lights winked on around the cabin. Holographic displays sprang to life around Schist, and the ship itself started to rumble as the engines came online.

Schist flicked a holo-control and spoke for the benefit of the listening hangar deck operators. "*Dark Dragon One* is ready for launch, over."

"Launch when ready, *DarkDragon One,*" said a woman's voice over the com.

Schist massaged a different holo-control, and the ship let out a dragon's roar that still sent a chill up Angar's spine. *RAAAAHHHHH! AYEEEEKKK!*

Grinning, he flipped his way through controls on the holo displays and physical console alike. "Hold on to your helmet, Horde Lord! Launching!"

Then, he smacked a red button in the middle of the console. *Dark Dragon One* lifted off smoothly, glided up to the hangar bay doorway, and shot into space like a bullet.

Or a dragon leaping out of its aerie.

CHAPTER 29

JUNGLEWORLD

WAVE AFTER WAVE OF NARL, COSSITORA, AND SKINDLE poured over the metal transmitter dish from all directions, firing energy weapons at the Gossa gathered near its center. There were dozens of attackers, at least, blasting away on the march, a multitude compared to the dozen or so Gossa they targeted.

Yet the armed warriors with their Caul-designed weapons proved to be no match for the Gossa shifters. Several of the Gossa formed a perimeter and turned into living walls capable of deflecting energy bolts. That drew the Caul soldiers in closer, concentrating their fire in the hope of breaking through—which was right where the Gossa wanted them. All at once, Gossa shifters leaped over the walls, transforming into massive creatures with reflective hides, studded with fangs and claws. They tore through the Narl and their allies with ferocious ease, shredding them in a flurry of blood and bone. With the front ranks decimated, they moved out from the center of the dish, ripping their way through the next line of the formation and the ones after that.

The air was filled with their blood-curdling roars and the agonized shrieks of their victims. Even Tork, a man who was no stranger to battles and suffering, thought it was an especially brutal performance.

He and Rogg remained at the center of the dish, protected behind the living walls of Gossa. The shifters wanted to keep Tork safe out of gratitude for his switching off the Song, and Rogg, as the one who knew him best, had been tapped to serve as his bodyguard.

"They just keep coming." Rogg had literally stuck his neck out, stretching it to great heights to take in the view over the walls. He retracted it now, returning his obsidian body to its normal proportions. "But my people are *slaughtering* them."

Tork paced inside the perimeter with battleax in hand, longing to fight yet disturbed at the same time. He was just starting to wonder if the situation was different than what he'd thought it was.

"I think they can do it, Rogg," he said. "I think they can kill every invader on the planet."

"'They'?" Rogg's ruby eyes flared.

"You," said Tork. "All of you. The Caul and their people don't stand a chance against you."

Rogg nodded. "They should never have hurt us. They *knew* what would happen."

The screams and sounds of rending flesh and breaking

bone rose to a crescendo beyond the living wall. "Because the Gossa have punished countless species before, you mean?" asked Tork.

"*Everyone* knows what happens if you try to control or abuse us." Rogg pointed at the walls and the ongoing battle beyond them. "We have destroyed *so* many peoples and planets for what they've done to us."

"And you'll do it again, won't you? That's what the others said."

"We can do it, too," said Rogg. "Now that the Song is gone, our minds are free in *every* way. We possess *vast* intelligence...more than enough to go where we like and exact our vengeance as we choose."

"Even against the Caul?" asked Tork.

Rogg snorted. "We have faced worse than them, I assure you. In the end, we have *always* triumphed."

"By wiping out entire *species*?" said Tork. "Even the innocents who never did you any wrong?"

"There *are* no innocents," snapped Rogg. "*You* know that. Just collateral damage."

A fresh round of agonized screams rose from beyond the wall. Somewhere out there, it sounded like someone was being tortured, shrieking with more intense pain with each passing moment.

"So you believe that every member of a species is equally responsible for the crimes of a few?" asked Tork.

"They are *complicit.*"

"Even if they had no idea the crimes were happening in the first place?"

Suddenly, Rogg shifted into a huge, hairy beast with fanged maws for eyes and teeth of flame. He towered over Tork and pounded his chest with gleaming black hooves.

"A price must be paid by all! There can be no exceptions!" He pounded his chest again and roared his anger at the sky. "An example must be set, or the persecution will never stop coming! My people have learned this the hard way!"

"I see." Tork nodded thoughtfully. "And how will you do it? How will you eradicate all these species?" He gestured at the wall, indicating the Caul fighters beyond it.

"We will go to their homeworlds and *destroy* them," said Rogg. "Not one of their people will be left *alive* when we have finished with them."

"Okay," said Tork. "And how are you going to get there, did you say?"

"We will use their own ships against them!" As if to emphasize the drama of his point, Rogg expanded his form again, doubling in size and growing jagged spines all over his body. "They are parked in this very base, fueled and ready for us to launch!"

"So as soon as your people are done fighting, they'll go right for the ships?"

"The sooner, the better," said Rogg. "Striking hard and fast is the best way to end a threat."

"I can't argue with that." Tork smiled. "So instead of standing around here being useless, maybe you and I should go liberate those ships and get them ready for blastoff?"

The screams got louder again, and Rogg seemed torn. He looked around as blood splashed over the walls and scorched and slashed-up body parts flew overhead. Tork thought he looked like he wanted to join the action.

Finally, then, he became a giant birdlike creature with a jagged bill and blood-red plumage. His wingspan, fully deployed, would have accommodated seven Torks lined up end to end.

"It's a good idea," he said, his voice a throaty croak. "The sooner those ships are ready to go, the sooner the Gossa's crusade can begin."

Grinning, Tork thrust his axe overhead and shook it in the pelting rain that had started up again. "Then let us ready the way for that crusade, as only you and I can!"

"The Great Gossa and Super Starbarian, off on another mission together!" shouted Rogg. "We *cannot* fail!"

"That's right!" Again, Tork pumped his axe in the air.

"Now jump on, Victim Eater!" Rogg bobbed his head, indicating Tork should climb up on his back. "Let's kill them all!"

"Kill them all!" said Tork as he crawled onto the giant bird and it took flight…though his true intentions, which he kept to himself, were not quite the same as Rogg's.

CHAPTER 30

Dark Dragon One

IT WAS HARD TO BELIEVE THAT MOMENTS AGO, SPACE around the jungle planet had been free of combat. Now, as Angar watched the display screens on the console aboard *Dark Dragon One*, all-out war was all he saw.

Fighters from the *Hellcyon* went after Caul alliance ships in orbit, blowing holes in one fuselage after another with their high-powered energy weapons. They had the advantage for the moment, as the Caul ships had all their guns pointing at the planet and couldn't turn them around fast enough to fend off the first round of strikes.

The advantage didn't last, as Caul ships spun and turned their guns away from the planet. When they made the turn, though, they saw a new enemy racing toward them with weapons blazing—an enemy with a great horned skull on its prow, eyes blazing with ruby light.

"*Hellcyon*'s coming in," said Schist as he flew *Dark Dragon One* smoothly through space behind the first wave of fighters. "And there's our window."

He pointed at a radar image hovering in midair between them. The image showed dozens of enemy ships surrounding the planet, mixed in with smaller fighter craft, plus the *Hellcyon*—and a narrow corridor with no traffic whatsoever, stretching from orbit to the surface of the planet. It opened as the enemy fleet was drawn to confront *Hellcyon*, leaving that one unobstructed sliver for some enterprising pilot to exploit.

Schist's hands flew over the controls, and *Dark Dragon One* whipped around and swooped toward the corridor. Angar pictured its sleek, black body flashing gracefully through the starry darkness, passing through the ranks of enemy gunboats and destroyers with their weapons all pointed in another direction.

Meanwhile, *Hellcyon* opened fire with its big guns, raining down bolts of destructive energy on whatever enemy ships were in range. One ship fired back immediately, only to be cracked open like an egg by *Hellcyon*'s powerful cannons. More ships in the enemy fleet followed, exploding or at least rupturing and leaking fuel, atmosphere, cargo…personnel.

Throughout it all, the *Hellcyon* fighter squadrons zipped and fired like swarming bees, punching holes in enemy ships and leaping away to their next targets with nimble grace. Sometimes, two or three fighters harried bigger ships together, darting between energy weapon bolts and tagging the fuselage so many times, they left them drifting derelicts.

"Hold on tight, Horde Lord," said Schist as he continued his rapid-fire assault on the control console. "This could be a wild ride when that window starts to close. Things are so chaotic up here, it won't stay open for long."

"Understood." Angar nodded once, bracing himself for the flight.

"Just stay focused on that link," said Schist. "Keep your bead on Tork and help guide me in. We need to zero in as fast as we..."

Suddenly, something hit *Dark Dragon One* hard, pitching it to one side. Another impact followed, gashing open the hull.

"Helmet!" shouted Schist in the last of the atmosphere gushing out of the hole.

Angar reached for his helmet, which he'd hung from a hook on the bulkhead—but it was just out of reach. Hastily, he unsnapped his harness, holding on to the couch with one hand and stretching behind him with the other. Donning the helmet was unnecessary, he didn't need air to breathe, but he wanted to at least pretend that wasn't the case for Schist's benefit.

Another jolt knocked the helmet off its hook, and it was sucked out into space. Angar made a half-hearted grab, coming up empty—and another jolt broke his grip on the back of the couch. Before he could grab hold of something else, the force of depressurization hauled him across the cockpit, tumbling toward the opening.

Then, he was spinning into space, unprotected, in the middle of the shootout with the forces of the Caul.

CHAPTER 31

JUNGLEWORLD

AT FIRST, NO ONE ROSE UP TO OPPOSE TORK AND THE GIANT bird creature when they landed on the tarmac of the Caul's spaceport, not far from the transmitter dish. Tork saw ranks of Narl, Cossitora, and Skindle charging past on their way to the dish to fight the Gossa, but none of them even seemed to notice that he and Rogg were among the parked spacecraft.

"Nice flying," said Tork. "Too bad we couldn't unscramble your powers sooner. It would've made our lives easier."

"That was a Keezo, a bird from my homeworld." Rogg sounded proud. "I won a prize once for shifting into the perfect Keezo, you know."

"Nice." Tork smiled and nodded. "I'll bet you can change into *anything* now."

Rogg shifted out of the bird form then and became what looked like a huge ball of writhing red snakes giving off a rancid blue smoke.

Immediately, he cried out and changed back to his blocky, obsidian self. "*That* wasn't supposed to happen! I guess I'm still a little rusty, after all."

Tork patted his head and laughed. For a moment, it was like Rogg was still his bumbling sidekick and meant no harm to innocents on faraway worlds.

"So there's something I've been wondering about," said Tork. "Is this your original form?"

This time, it was Rogg's turn to laugh. "Not even close! It's a species of rock people called the Vark. They invaded my homeworld a while back."

"Then what *is* your natural state?" asked Tork.

"Outsiders can never see it," said Rogg. "But *you* have. You just didn't realize it at the time."

"What?!" Tork's eyes flew wide open. "Where? What was it?"

"I'll never tell," Rogg said with a chuckle.

Even with chaos raging nearby, they managed to share that moment as if nothing had changed. It might be the last such moment they would have, given what lay on the horizon.

The time they'd spent together in the jungle and the battles they'd fought had forged a friendship between them. That bond had reenergized Tork after being so long alone, even if Rogg had been using him all along to achieve his people's goals.

Their connection had gotten him through tough times.

It would make what he planned to do next all the more difficult.

But it had to be done. That was the one thing Tork was sure of.

"So let's get these ships ready for blastoff," said Rogg. "My people will be ready for them soon. It won't take long for them to finish off the invaders on the ground."

"I think you're right." Tork heard the screams hit a feverish peak down in the dish...but none of the screams were Gossa. Whatever the shifters were doing out there in the wreckage and rain, it must have been awful indeed to inspire such cries from seasoned fighters. "We'd better get busy, then."

Rogg turned his back and walked off between the rows of sleek spacecraft parked on the tarmac. "Follow me," he said. "Let's put our time to good use for the cause of the Gossa."

"All right." As Tork followed, he drew the axe from his back and wrapped both hands around its handle. He knew what he had to do was right—that demolishing the ships was the only way to save multitudes of innocents on faraway planets. He also knew if Rogg was an obstacle to that goal, he had to remove him.

"Here. This looks like a good place to start." With that, Rogg scooted around the nose of a ship up ahead, disappearing behind the fuselage.

Tork walked along that ship's length, raising the axe for what would come next.

"One thing I can't figure out, though," said Rogg. "Care to explain?"

"Explain what?" said Tork.

Suddenly, Rogg burst from behind the nose of the ship, his body transformed into a 12-foot-tall lizard beast with emerald scales and a fanged maw that breathed out fire.

"Care to explain how you plan to get *spacecraft* ready to launch when you don't even know how to fly a damn *plane* without autopilot?"

His words were followed by a burst of flame that sizzled straight toward Tork.

CHAPTER 32

*IN SPACE, **Near Dark Dragon One***

ANGAR TUMBLED THROUGH AIRLESS, FREEZING SPACE without a helmet, watching the damaged *Dark Dragon One* get further and further away.

To a normal man, it would have been a death sentence. Even without needing to breathe air, Angar should have died fast from exposure to the cold and vacuum.

But Angar was even less of a normal man than he'd known. Not only did he not asphyxiate from lack of air, but he didn't freeze, and his body didn't puff up from nitrogen bubbles expanding under the skin.

He just kept tumbling, completely aware and functional, no more damaged than if he'd been sitting under a tree on a sunny day. Nothing inside him exploded or shut down.

And that wasn't even the most amazing part of his spacewalk.

As he fell, he saw an enemy ship draw close to *Dark Dragon One*—a fighter, perhaps the very craft that had blown open the dragon's hull. The fighter's guns were aimed directly at the drifting hulk, swiftly approaching point blank range.

Angar's heart pounded as the fighter's guns charged, twinkling with energy ready to be released. Clearly, the pilot was moving in to finish off the dragon with one last barrage of energy bolts. Major Schist, who was still inside, would be destroyed along with it.

And Angar was too far away to do anything about it.

Rage burned within him at the thought of it—not only losing his friend, but his hope of retrieving Tork as well. And if he and Tork were lost, the future of the galaxy would be lost, too. The Blacksmiths and the Undoing would not stand a chance against the Caul without their two secret weapons.

So consumed was Angar with these furious thoughts, he did not at first realize when his situation suddenly changed. It took a moment for him to register that he wasn't spinning uncontrollably away from *Dark Dragon One* anymore.

Given the laws of physics as explained by Isabel, he should not have stopped spinning unless some other force had acted upon him. Furthermore, it should have been impossible for him to propel himself back the way he'd come, sailing toward the dragon without assistance.

Yet that was exactly what he did.

Without understanding why it happened, Angar

crossed the gulf of space, gathering speed as he got closer to the enemy fighter. The pilot must not have seen him coming, because the fighter's guns never strayed from the dragon. Their charge continued to build, and they would blow the hell out of the ship and Major Schist at any moment.

At least, they would have done that if Angar hadn't plowed into the fighter first, ramming it away from *Dark Dragon One*. The guns still fired, but their bolts shot harmlessly into space.

The fighter's thrusters fired as the pilot fought to keep his ship from drifting too far from the dragon. He swung the fighter around and back, teeing up the guns for another attack.

But Angar was already leaping onto the fuselage in front of the cockpit. Letting out a silent roar, he slammed his fists down on the clear cowling of the cockpit, unleashing every bit of strength at his disposal.

Not only did the blow not hurt a bit, but it cracked the cowling.

Angar didn't waste time wondering how it was possible. Instead, he kept pounding away with both fists, causing a spiderweb of cracks to spread through the transparent material. The pilot, meanwhile, did what he could to dislodge him—spinning the fighter around, bucking it up and down, flipping it up over.

But Angar wasn't about to let go. He just kept hanging on and hammering away, determined to end the threat.

Then, suddenly, the cowling shattered, and the cockpit atmosphere rushed out into space. Angar thrust his hands inside, swatting away the pilot's pistol—then hauling out the Skindle pilot, snapping his harness in pieces, and heaving him off into space.

The pilot wore an environment suit and survived, but his flight was uncontrollable. Within seconds, his constant speed carried him far away, tumbling toward the planet with no means of reversing course.

With the pilot out of the way and the fighter disabled, Angar swooped back to the derelict dragon. He stopped at the gash in the hull and squeezed inside, returning to what was now an airless cabin.

Once inside, he turned and grabbed both sides of the hull around the hole. Straining, he pulled the sides together and pinched the hole shut. Then, without thinking, he did something else he'd never done before.

He stared at the pinched seam until ruby red beams of energy flashed out of his eyes, welding it together.

From the middle to the top, then down to the bottom, he fused the rippled seam with blistering heat. Only then, with the cabin sealed against the void, did he move to check on Schist, who was slumped over the control console.

He couldn't tell from looking if the crystalline man was alive or dead—but he held out hope. Like Angar, Schist didn't need to breathe air; mineral-based being that he was, Angar guessed he could survive in space, too.

Angar shook him by the shoulder, but there was no response. Schist's crystalline head had a gray pallor he hadn't seen before, though maybe that just meant he was unconscious.

Angar shook him again, harder—then a third time that did the trick. Schist stirred, the color of his crystalline form changing from gray to blue. He looked groggily at Angar, then pushed himself up and started working the controls on the console at rapid-fire speed.

Lights flicked on around the cabin, and display screens flashed back to life. Air hissed back in from backup tanks as life support returned to the ship.

Finally, there was enough air in the cabin to carry sound. Angar knew it when he could hear himself clearing his throat.

"All systems...returning to full power," said Schist. "No damage to the engines...fortunately."

"Good to know." Angar lowered himself onto his flight couch and snapped the harness back into place around him.

"Hull integrity is also one hundred percent." Schist looked back at the welded seam between sections of the bulkhead without comment.

"Sounds like we're in good shape," said Angar. "Good enough to complete our mission?"

Schist checked displays and readouts across the board, examined a hologram of the ship's projected course to the planet, tapped a finger against his lower lip in thought. "Hell yes," he said at last. "The window's still open, as well."

Angar clapped his hands together and grinned. "Then what are we waiting for?"

Schist looked back at the welded seam again, frowning —then returned his full attention to the console. "Absolutely nothing."

With that, he punched a big, red button on the board, and *Dark Dragon One* lunged toward the planet's atmosphere.

CHAPTER 33

JUNGLEWORLD

TORK BOLTED, AND THE BLAST OF FLAME MISSED, SINGEING the nose of one of the parked spacecraft instead.

Axe in hand, he kept running between the rows of ships, staying out of range of the next fiery attack...also figuring out a strategy to take down Rogg before Rogg took him down first.

He still couldn't believe Rogg had gotten the drop on him, transforming into a 12-foot-tall, firebreathing lizard beast and going in for the kill. Finally rid of the Song's debilitating influence, the Gossa sidekick was a formidable enemy.

Was Rogg up for killing his former partner if he had the chance? The way he was coming after Tork, murderous intent seemed like a distinct possibility.

"Come out and let's get this over with!" shouted Rogg. "Don't you want to see if you can beat me?"

Tork darted between two ships, ending up in another row. He paused there a moment to think, even as Rogg's heavy footsteps stomped ever closer to his position.

Fighting the shifter could be a serious challenge, now that Rogg was in full command of his powers. A truce made more sense, but Tork couldn't imagine it would happen. Rogg had made the first move, after all, and it had been a murderous one.

There would be no easy way out of this confrontation.

"Come on, Starbarian!" Rogg sounded closer than ever, on the other side of the rows of ships. "Don't tell me you're worried you can't *beat* me?"

Tork drew a deep breath, preparing for battle. It would be better to get it over with, he thought, and get to work sabotaging as many ships as he could before the other Gossa showed up.

Gripping the axe tightly, he jogged between ships, following Rogg's voice. He finally emerged in the row where he knew Rogg would be, ready for anything.

Except Rogg wasn't there.

"What the *shang?*" Tork looked all around, but there was no sign of his traveling partner—just ships and tarmac and pouring rain.

Then, suddenly, the rain attacked.

A sheet of falling water leaped out at him, blasting him with enough watery force to knock the axe from his grip and toss him to the ground. As Tork fell, scrambling to regain his footing, Rogg changed from pelting rain to an oversized version of his default obsidian form—a seven-foot-tall rock creature with the same glowing ruby eyes as the smaller original. Before Tork could swing his axe, the stony giant landed a massive fist square in his gut.

The blow hit like a ton of rubble, sending a wave of white hot agony rolling through Tork. It left him reeling on the tarmac, fighting to push past the pain—even as Rogg pulled the stone fist back for another strike.

Tork rolled out of the way at the last second, and the fist crashed into the tarmac. Springing to his feet, he scooped up the axe, thumbed on the power, and heaved it back in one smooth gesture...then swung it with all his strength at Rogg.

The blade bounced off Rogg's stony hide with a resounding *clang*. As soon as he'd deflected it, Rogg trans-formed himself to match it, changing from a rock creature into one made entirely of gleaming, electrified metal.

He turned out to be magnetic, too. When Tork took his next swing, the flat side of the blade lurched over and stuck to Rogg's chest. Tork grabbed at the handle, trying to wrench it free, and Rogg swatted him away with a casual backhand swipe.

Tork had barely landed against the body of a nearby ship when Rogg leaped at him with both arms upraised and reshaped like the blade of the axe. They both sliced deep into his torso, pinning him to the tarmac as the blood poured out of him.

Tork gulped and twitched like a dying fish. He felt the life rush out in a wave of intense heat followed by the iciest cold he's ever experienced.

"Sorry it had to be like this, Starbarian." Rogg sounded genuinely sorry as he retracted his axe blade hands from the massive gouges they'd made. "But I can't let you stand in our way. There are scores that must be settled."

"Even...the innocents?" gasped Tork.

"You *know* there's no such thing," said Rogg. "There's only *us* and *them*."

Just as Rogg uttered those words, a familiar darkness swept through Tork, wiping away everything that made him who he was. His mind was rendered blank, his senses inert, as his very presence was extinguished from existence.

He breathed his last, rattling breath in the rain.

"I'll miss you, Starbarian." Rogg took on Tork's blond-haired form, knelt beside him, and smiled, rolling Tork's eyelids shut over his dead green eyes. "Thanks again for freeing my people."

He leaned close, intending to kiss Tork's forehead. That was when Tork's eyes suddenly flung wide open.

And Tork butted him so hard with his head, it sent him toppling to the tarmac.

Tork grinned and leaped to his feet. "Some friend *you* are!" Then, he pounced on his onetime ally, fully healed from Rogg's attack and invigorated in every possible way. Once again, he'd returned from the dead, and he didn't want to repeat the process anytime soon.

CHAPTER 34

Dark Dragon One

ANGAR GRIPPED THE ARMS OF THE FLIGHT COUCH AS *DARK Dragon One* streaked toward the surface of the jungle planet. The ship shook so violently, it felt like it was going to rattle apart—but it held together in spite of the stress of descent. Even with a makeshift welded seam in a cockpit bulkhead, the *Dragon* remained intact as it rocketed through the turbulent atmosphere.

The whole time, Angar clung to the thread of his link with Tork, sensing the signal of his life like a beacon down below...at least until it was suddenly cut short.

No! His indrawn breath hissed between clenched teeth. *Not when you're so close!*

He wanted to leap from the dragon and fly at high speed to rescue Tork, but he had no idea if his powers would work as well in the atmosphere as in space. Riding the rest of the way down with Schist was his only real choice, even if he already knew the journey would be for nothing in the end.

"Major Schist." He started to tell the pilot what had happened and what it meant...

...only to feel his connection to Tork suddenly blaze back to life.

"What is it?" asked Schist.

"Nothing. Just..." Angar pointed at the central display screen, which showed the planet's surface rapidly getting closer. "Keep going that way. I can feel him."

"Good to know." Schist nodded and hit more controls. The ship hurtled like a dropped stone, then leveled out above the tops of the trees in the jungle. "Got directions on a landing site?"

Up ahead, Angar saw smoke rising from a vast clearing in the midst of the jungle. The clearing was occupied by a complex of white-walled buildings, plus a massive silver dish set into a central hilltop.

A zoomed-in shot showed a battle in progress on that dish, a struggle between Caul allies and a group of strange beings who constantly changed shape and fought like maniacs.

"Head for *that*." Angar tapped the screen displaying the battle scene with his fingertip. "It's just a *gut feeling*, of course."

"Of course." Smirking, Schist turned the wheel, and the ship banked hard to port. "You and your damn gut feelings."

On one of the screens that showed more zoomed-out views, Angar spotted another fight happening among the ranks of spaceships parked on a vast, paved launchpad. "Wait, what's that?" He pointed at the scene on the screen. From a distance, it looked like a huge insect creature slugging it out with a human being. "Where's it happening?"

Schist played with controls and stared at readouts on the console. "Less than half a mile from the fight in the big dish."

Angar frowned, focusing in on the signal. It was stronger than ever, leaving no doubt it was coming from the fight on the launchpad.

"That's it, all right," he said tensely. "That's where he is."

"Then I guess we better get down there," said Schist. "Don't wanna miss out on the action, do we?"

"Nope." Angar reached for his sword and checked the settings on the hilt. Everything had been leading up to this battle, and he needed to make sure he was ready.

"I'll put her down near those ships," said Schist. "There's just one problem."

Angar flicked the sword's power on, then off, then on again. "What's that?"

"Reinforcements." Schist pointed at a screen where an aerial image of the ground below was visible. From what Angar could see, the launchpad was completely surrounded by a ring of fast-approaching attackers. "An army of them."

Angar took in the view, then shrugged and went back to readying his blade. "Good," he said. "I could use a little workout."

CHAPTER 35

JUNGLEWORLD

COULD TORK COME BACK TO LIFE IF HE WAS BEHEADED? IT was a question he had no desire to put to the test.

That was why, as the giant claw swung his way, he leaped upward. Rogg, in the form of a giant green mantis creature, had already shown what that claw could do, slicing the nose off a nearby spacecraft with one stroke. Now it was heading straight for Tork's neck—and Tork was compelled to leap out of its path.

What he didn't expect, however, was just how far his leap would take him. He soared straight up, passing the tops of the jungle trees before he ran out of momentum.

When he reached the peak of his jump, he grinned and took in the view, just for an instant—just before gravity hauled him back down toward the tarmac.

Deciding to put his fall to good use, he quickly spun around so he was falling headfirst, aimed right at the giant mantis with his axe held out in front of him. He came down hard, driving the blade of the axe through the middle of the monster bug's head, dredging up a fountain of bright green goo.

The mantis roared and tossed its head, but Tork held on tight by the handle of his axe. Rogg finally shook him by changing shape, becoming a cloud of noxious mist that no one could cling to.

The axe dropped through the cloud with no resistance, its blade stabbing into the tarmac—bringing Tork along so fast, he flipped over when it hit and lost his grip on the weapon.

The mist quickly coalesced into a massive, long-necked dinosaur thing. It raised a foreleg high, intending to crush him—its foot so huge, it would dwarf him when it fell.

Tork thought he could get out from under in time, but the foot dropped faster than expected. Seized by desperation and a surge of adrenaline, he braced himself and flung up his hands.

And the massive foot stopped dead without even touching him.

He still felt the weight of it pressing toward him, fighting whatever he was doing to keep it aloft. Without understanding how he was able to do what he'd done, he instinctively pushed back with all his strength, casting up a wave of force that threw the foot off so hard, it flipped the entire dinosaur on its back.

Tork was stunned but had no time consider how he'd

gotten his new edge. As soon as Rogg the dinosaur flipped over, smashing the tarmac under him, he transformed into Rogg the jet-black, dome-headed xenomorph, a slime-dripping, two-legged beast with a long tail and bony exoskeleton.

Rogg sprang, ejecting a second set of jaws from his mouth, making a sound like a screeching cat. Eager to try his own trick again, Tork swung up his hands and concentrated with all his might on holding the beast at bay.

He succeeded. Rogg froze, just a few yards away, then flew off at a high rate of speed, spinning like a propeller as he went. He screeched louder than ever as he collided with a big cruiser, impaling on an energy weapon mounted on one of the wings.

Even that, Tork knew, wouldn't hold him for long. Running over to his axe, he considered trying his power on it, then decided just to tear it free of the tarmac with his own brute physical strength.

As he was doing so, he heard the first blasts from above.

Drawn by the sound, he whirled toward it—and was doubly shocked. In the distance, gouts of flame were raining down on an army of creatures shifting rapidly between all shapes and sizes. He'd been so wrapped up in his fight with Rogg until then that he hadn't even known the Gossa hordes were closing in.

But what shocked him the most was the source of the fiery tongues. He couldn't believe his eyes and had to squint to be sure what he saw.

But in the end, he was sure. The sound of its cries, even from far away, confirmed it.

RAAAAHHHHH! AYEEEEKKK!

The great black dragon that he and Angar had fought in the contest back on Earth was flying toward him, blasting away multitudes of shapeshifters with gust after gust of its fiery breath.

CHAPTER 36

Dark Dragon One

IT WAS LIKE FACING THE DENIZENS OF HELL ITSELF, TEN thousand demons constantly changing into endlessly different and more dangerous forms.

Angar had never seen anything like it. As he watched the shapeshifting army on the display screens, he was transfixed by the madness of it all, the constant, ravenous churn. He wondered how it would feel to confront that horde face to face, even with the new powers that had come to him in orbit.

And he wondered how in Yorg's name Tork had survived for so long on a planet populated by things like *that.*

"So much for the element of surprise." Schist was leaning forward, hyper-focused on the controls and displays on his console. "Damn things are coming after us."

Watching the screens, Angar saw beings from the horde sprout wings and lift off, flapping their way toward the *Dark Dragon One.* Each one was a fresh horror right out of a nightmare, complete with horns or claws or tentacles or spines or all of the above. A few breathed fire of their own clouds of acid or explosive fumes.

"I'm trying to burn them as soon as they leave the ground." *Dark Dragon One* lurched as Schist swung it around and unleashed a burst of hellfire, roasting a flock of pursuers. "But there are just too many of them."

Something thudded against the ship. Angar moved to jump out of his seat, but Schist reached over and held him back.

"Relax, I've got this." Schist spun the wheel, and the dragon executed a barrel roll. Whatever had latched onto the ship scratched and bumped its way over the hull and dropped off.

Angar held on tight with one hand and kept his sword clamped firmly in the other. Just as the ship leveled out, he saw something else hurtle toward it on the screen—what looked like an enormous brain with wings like a vulture.

Many more creatures were soaring close behind.

"They just keep coming." Schist's voice was beyond tense. "So much for the idea of blasting ourselves some breathing room."

Angar took a good look at all the video and said something he'd never said before in his life. "This is a war we can't win."

"Correct." Schist unleashed more flame and swooped

the ship away from the nightmarish ranks rising to meet it. "That just means we have less time to get Tork out of here."

Angar felt the ship move faster, leaving the front lines of the shape changers behind. Up ahead, he saw a tiny human figure battling what looked like a mishmash of different forms merged into a single huge sphere.

"That's him up there, right?" asked Schist.

Angar didn't need the link anymore to recognize Tork. "That's him."

Again, the ship accelerated. "Then let's go get him. Get ready to help him fight off that thing down there."

"Ready." Angar rose from his seat with sword firmly in hand. "And I can't wait to see his face when I show him how it's done...*again.*"

CHAPTER 37

JUNGLEWORLD

TORK'S HEART HAMMERED WITH JOY AT THE SIGHT OF THE great black dragon ship roasting Gossa forces with its fiery breath. If the dragon was here, it meant the Blacksmiths had finally found him and were not far behind. It meant he finally had hope of escaping Jungleworld and returning to the larger war at hand.

Unfortunately, Rogg wouldn't let him dwell on the positive development for long. The determined shifter raced back to him in a bizarre spherical shape, a combination of body parts melded together. They looked like they were all from different species and couldn't possibly function in that state—yet they flung out fists and feet and tusks and claws that looked every bit as deadly as a jumbled agglomeration.

Thrusting a hand in front of him, Tork focused his

mind on breaking up the sphere of body parts. An entire layer of limbs and organs fell away, flopping on the tarmac—but the core of the thing kept coming, and in fact picked up speed. It reached him in seconds, grabbing and stabbing and clawing, seeking to tear him apart.

Tork shifted gears fast, giving up on the mind force and hacking away with the axe instead. Every time some extension of the sphere reached for him, he chopped it off, sending it bouncing to the tarmac.

When it got there, other body parts squirmed and slithered and crawled up to merge with it, absorbing it into another mass taking shape at Tork's feet.

"You might as well give up now," said a voice from within the larger sphere. *"You can never beat a shape-shifter!"*

Clenching his teeth, Tork kicked away a cluster of grasping hands and swung the axe at the hovering sphere. More parts fell away and joined together scrambling on the ground, even as Tork continued hacking with the axe.

When the severed body parts started coming after him more aggressively from the tarmac, he started to wonder if Rogg might be right. How could you fight something that came back to life deadlier than before every time you took a piece out of it?

"I won't let you stop my people from having their revenge," said Rogg. *"I'll do whatever it takes!"*

"So will I!" Tork plunged his blade deep in the twitching, twisting sphere, then pried open a wedge of limbs and maws and tails. As he did so, a long, rubbery tentacle stretched out of the mass and wrapped itself around his throat.

The tentacle tightened fast, jolting him into the mass

so hard, he let go of the axe. As soon as he got close enough, dozens of other extremities from as many different species took hold of him, pulling him deeper inside.

The tentacle's stranglehold cut off the flow of blood to his brain, and darkness crowded his vision. He tried to fight, but he couldn't focus enough to use his mind or body to fend off the assault.

As the darkness rushed in, he felt himself slipping away. The fact that he'd come back from the dead before did nothing to stave off the wave of fear and dismay that coursed through him as the end loomed.

"Goodbye, Starbarian." Rogg's voice seemed to come from a thousand miles away. *"I promise to put your face and body to good use while you're gone."*

Tork thrashed one last time, then stopped moving. His grip on life grew looser and looser...

Then, suddenly, he was dragged back out of the darkness and thrown into the light again.

Someone shook him roughly, and each new shake brought him closer to awareness. He covered the last distance with one giant leap, and his eyes sprang wide open all at once.

It was only then, seeing the grinning face before him, that he realized who had saved him. *"Angar?"*

The Horde Lord who'd rescued him laughed. *"Starbarian? Since when are you a Starbarian?"*

CHAPTER 38

JUNGLEWORLD

"I can't believe you found me!" said Tork. "I can't believe you're here!"

"Neither can I," Angar said sarcastically. "Nice beard, by the way."

"*Shang* you!" Tork looked around at the remains of Rogg, which were scattered all over the tarmac. The hunks of flesh were charred black, as if they'd been cooked in an open fire. "And I didn't need help beating the *shapeshifter*, you know."

"My mistake," said Angar. "I guess you don't need help with *them*, either?" He hiked a thumb in the direction of the Gossa army charging over the tarmac toward them.

"You're not so dumb after all." Tork stepped away to retrieve his axe. It was covered with bits of exploded Rogg, and he brushed them off with the side of his hand.

"Though I guess I wouldn't mind if you wanted to help blow up all these ships here."

Angar walked over to one of the nearby ships and rapped on the metal fuselage. "This wouldn't have anything to do with the pissed-off shapeshifters, would it?"

"Yes, it would," said Tork. "As soon as they get done with killing everyone they hate here, they want to do the same out there." He pointed straight up.

Angar nodded and tapped his earlobe, activating his commlink. "Schist?" He tried again. "Schist, where are you?"

When he got no reply, he turned and scanned the sky above the approaching Gossa army. He soon spotted *Dark Dragon One*, but its situation wasn't great. The ship was covered with shapeshifters in various guises, making it wobble and buck and flounder.

Meaning Angar and Tork's escape route was cut off for the moment, just as a massive army of shapeshifting beings was closing in with murderous intent.

"Remember how you always said you wanted to die in battle?" Angar swung his sword in a lazy figure eight overhead.

"I never said that." Tork stood beside him, watching the Gossa army tear toward them. Multiple figures rose from the crowd on wings and flew out ahead, flapping hard to reach their targets first. "One thing I *do* know is, those bastards don't stand a chance."

"That's the spirit." Angar pointed at *Dark Dragon One*, which was still bobbing in midair, covered with demonic shifters who were pounding the hell out of it in multiple hostile forms. "So we need to get *that* ship free to destroy all of *those* ships and get *us* the *shang* off this mudball planet."

"Is *that* all?" Tork smirked as he spun his axe in a circle, then stopped with its blade pointed at the approaching mob. "No problem whatsoever. As long as *you* don't mind fighting beside an Easterner like me."

"The only problem I have is thinking I might not get back to the *Hellcyon* and tell everyone how I had to pull your *ass* out of the fire." Angar laughed.

"Yeah, that would be awful, wouldn't it?" There was sarcasm in Tork's voice. "So good luck to the both of us, Horde Lord."

"You too, 'Starbarian.' " Swinging his sword, Angar marched off with shoulders squared to meet the oncoming army of screaming, shifting maniacs.

Tork strode alongside him, eyes glinting at the nearness of battle. "Starbarian yourself, Angar."

CHAPTER 39

JUNGLEWORLD

IT TOOK ONE DIVING HARPY SLASHING WITH RAZOR-SHARP claws to get Tork to put his powers to use.

For a hot second, he'd thought maybe he should conceal his powers from Angar and use the secret to his advantage later—but the slashing harpy and the monsters flying in behind her kicked that thought right out of his head.

Reaching deep, Tork projected a pulse of invisible force that struck the harpy dead-on. The winged beast screamed as its bones cracked and wings snapped from the impact. He used it as a battering ram, blasting it through the rank of flyers and setting off a chain reaction that knocked down a half-dozen of them.

Glancing in Angar's direction, he saw that he shouldn't have worried about revealing secret powers in the first place. As Angar hacked at dive-bombing flyers with his sword, twin red beams flashed from his eyes, burning holes in their bodies that left them shrieking in pain. When one of the beasts slung a massive metal fist at him, he shattered it with a single glancing blow from one of his own, blowing shrapnel in all directions.

So yes, Angar had gone through some changes, too. Keeping the kid gloves on made no sense at all.

Roaring a battle cry, Tork took the axe to an incoming winged creature, lopping off one of its three heads, then turning his mental force on the others. To his surprise, both heads exploded in crimson bursts, a result he hadn't known his powers could cause until then.

Looking up, he saw the dragon ship coming closer, still covered in flying shapeshifters. The shifters changed shape as he watched, turning their limbs into drills and spikes and hammers to batter the ship out of the sky. If they kept it up, he could tell it wouldn't last long.

Tork broke into a run, passing Angar as he fought a clutch of flyers. When two of the flyers turned and flapped toward Tork, he blew their heads apart and kept running.

Heart hammering, Tork charged forward as if he were about to feed himself into the meat grinder of the oncoming army. The Gossa howled with savage joy and rushed to meet him, some transforming into reptilian, cheetah-like creatures racing over the tarmac.

At the last second, though, Tork leaped up and over them all, aiming like a missile at the struggling *Dark Dragon One*. He came in feet-first, smashing the back of one of the beasts clinging to the ship. As the beast wailed in agony, Tork wrenched it free and tossed it aside, sending it tumbling into the raging crowd below.

From there, he worked his way around the fuselage, hacking shifters with his axe and blowing up or tearing them off with the force of his mind. One by one, whole or in pieces, they fell away from the dragon and disappeared in the murderous mob.

Finally, Tork stood alone on the hull, and the ship steadied…but the moment of peace didn't last. Tork heard sounds from below and leaned over the side to see what was causing them.

That was when he saw hordes of flying shifters take wing and rise out of the angry throng, heading directly for the dragon-ship. There were dozens of them, and the count didn't stop there.

More lifted off with each passing second.

CHAPTER 40

JUNGLEWORLD

ANGAR WONDERED IF HE COULD FLY ONLY THROUGH SPACE.

Looking up as he finished his latest battle with the shapeshifters on the ground, he saw that Tork had freed *Dark Dragon One*—but a vast flock of winged reinforcements were heading straight for him.

Even with the powers he'd seen Tork demonstrate—blowing up heads and leaping great heights—Angar doubted he could stave off *that* many attackers for long. Could he reach him in time to help hold the line?

In space, it would not have been a problem. Angar could soar up there, unaided—but could he do the same down here?

If he didn't try, the dragon-ship would soon be lost, and the army of shifters would overwhelm him with numbers and ferocity.

Breathing fast, he focused on channeling all his strength and will into getting off the ground. One of the shifters in lizard-cheetah form charged up and pounced, and Angar cut his throat with a flick of his sword while getting ready.

He killed another shifter—an inside-out gorilla thing glistening with slime—and crouched, coiling the muscles in his legs for the hoped-for launch.

Before the next pod of shifters could reach him, he pushed off the tarmac, straining for a skyward leap to carry him all the way to the *Dark Dragon One.* Instead, he only managed to hop a few inches off the pavement and came right back down.

"Shang!" Moments away from colliding with the next group, he concentrated even harder on reaching the heights—but again, couldn't gain any altitude.

Thinking fast, he decided he needed a bigger push... and he got an idea. Crouching again, he directed his gaze at the tarmac and focused on unleashing the energy beams from his eyes.

They held back at first, then hit the tarmac with sudden, explosive power. The blast of force propelled him upward, where his power of flight took over. Though he switched off the beams, he kept climbing and was able to control his course and speed, aiming for the mass of monsters heading for the dragon.

He entered their midst with sword flashing, carving up flying shifters of every description. They dropped like flies as he slashed up their bodies, leaving them with blood gushing and guts spilling out.

Clearing a path with fatal swipes of his blade, he

climbed a ladder of death toward the hovering *Dark Dragon One.* When he got close enough, he turned his eye beams on the creatures swarming the ship's underside, scalding them into releasing their grips.

Finally, he was able to grab onto the hull himself, seizing a handhold built into the ebon fuselage. He scaled the side and swung up to the top of the ship, finding what looked like a huge huddle of variegated creatures, working feverishly on some project he couldn't see.

Working on Tork, no doubt.

Sword in hand, he took a step toward them—then stopped as they fell away all at once, thrown aside by Tork with a single mighty flood of force.

Most of the shifters slid off the ship and hurtled toward the army on the ground, but a few dug in or stuck to the fuselage and took another shot at Tork. One by one, their heads exploded, and their bodies crumpled to the scaly black hull.

Angar knew what was coming next—more replacements, flapping up to continue the fight. With that vast army of eager volunteers, there would be an endless supply of them piling onto the ship.

At least as long as the ship continued to hover above them.

Running forward over the hull, Angar found the upper hatch and wrenched it open. He clambered down the ladder inside and dropped into the cockpit, instantly on guard for trouble.

That was when he found out why the ship was stuck in place, and Schist hadn't answered his com calls.

He heard the male voice of the ship's computer repeat

a message in urgent tones. *"Autopilot offline. Awaiting command to engage."*

Though Schist was still on his flight couch, he and the couch were engulfed by a shivering blob of pale pink protoplasm—a shifter that had slipped inside, no doubt. While Schist sat frozen amid that pink goo, multiple status lights on his console blinked steady yellow, indicating ship systems were locked in neutral.

If ever there were a perfect time to use optical energy beams, this was it.

Moving closer, Angar released the beams from his eyes, focusing them on the pink goop. As soon as the gelatinous gunk started to sizzle, it let out a screech of pain and slung out a pseudopod to try to take him down.

Angar simply shifted the energy beams to the pseudopod and turned up the gain as high as he could. The pseudopod's mass instantly melted, running onto the floor of the cabin like molten wax.

Before Angar could burn off the rest of the blob, it slithered off Schist's unconscious body and reformed, becoming a crablike thing with huge claws and mandibles. It came after him fast, its claws and jaws clacking viciously, leaving Schist on his own.

Grinning, Angar lunged his sword forward, planting it deep in the maw of the beast. Letting go of the hilt, he grabbed a mandible with each hand, bleeding around the serrated edges. Then, with one great surge of strength, he wrenched them apart so hard that he tore them right out of the creature's head.

Its claws went on clacking as it sank to the deck, its shape warping into something else on the way down. By the time it stopped twitching, it looked part-crab, part-bear, part-something completely unrecognizable, all equally defeated and dead.

Angar hopped over the mess and went straight to Schist. He shook him three times and shouted his name over the repeating message from the computer, trying to bring him around.

"Wake up, damnit! Come on!" He shook him again, more roughly than ever. "I need you! I can't fly this ship!"

Still, there was no reaction. Schist lolled on the flight couch, an inanimate crystalline figure, his facets without the slightest hint of healthy color.

That was when the computer's message changed.

"Command intervention required or systems failure in one minute."

Panic coursed through Angar. Though he didn't fully understand how the ship worked, he knew enough to comprehend the gist of the message.

He shook Schist again, to no avail…and then he had an idea. He thought of something he could try, something dangerous, maybe even stupid. For all he knew, it might just as easily kill Schist as wake him up.

"Command intervention required or systems failure in thirty seconds."

But trying it was the only card he had left to play. Closing his eyes, he concentrated on activating the energy beams but controlling their intensity. By keeping his eyes narrowed, he hoped to keep the beams just strong enough to shock Schist out of unconsciousness without melting or blasting his crystalline form.

Slowly, as he felt the heat of the beams build behind his lids, he started opening his eyes.

CHAPTER 41

JUNGLEWORLD

DARK DRAGON ONE WAS LOSING ALTITUDE, A LITTLE AT A time. Fighting off shifters from atop the ship, Tork could feel it slowly sinking. At the rate of its descent, it would be immersed in the shifter army soon enough.

Moments earlier, he'd seen Angar slip inside, but he must have failed to save the ship. Whatever had happened in there, nothing had changed.

Horde Lord that he was, Tork would fight to the end with every weapon and power at his disposal. He would make them pay dearly for every blow they struck, every bit of life they took from him.

His only regret was that he might fail to stop them from launching the Caul fleet into space on a bloody and indiscriminate campaign of revenge. Except for the few ships damaged in the battle so far, those spacecraft would not be disabled or destroyed, and the Gossa would be free to wreak havoc where they chose.

The dragon-ship dropped a little further, and more airborne Gossa piled on, determined to take it down. Their fierce caterwauling filled his ears as they scrambled toward him, out for blood.

He answered by charging into their midst with his battleaxe swinging, claiming lives like the scythe of a reaper.

The Gossa slashed and lashed and stabbed at him, only to have every blow deflected by invisible force or the application of muscular power. They tried to knock him over the edge or pluck him up from above or suffocate him with force of numbers, and he made their heads explode.

Still, *Dark Dragon One* dropped lower.

When he'd finished clearing the deck again, Tork stood for a moment, preparing for the next wave—preparing also for a final descent that could come at any time. Drenched in sweat and rain, he wondered if there were limits to his resurrection power...if he could still revive if torn to tiny pieces by a blood-crazed mob. Could his body reassemble? Or would his consciousness be restored but scattered among the tiny bits?

He quickly realized he was about to find out. *Dark Dragon One* lurched downward, plunging like an elevator toward the thousands of grasping claws and tentacles in the crowd.

Tork braced himself, gripping the axe tightly with both hands. Strangely enough, he thought of Scalder Pacious back on Earth during the Raider Wars. He wondered if dying like this for a noble cause could redeem him for the mistakes he'd made that had cost Scalder his life.

Maybe, in the end, it was up to him to decide.

The howling of the shifters raced toward him, the battle of his life flashing near…and then the ship jolted to a stop so sudden, it almost knocked him over.

Tork felt the dragon shiver as it hung there for a moment, just out of reach of the Gossa throng. Then, a stronger vibration surged through the fuselage, building in intensity with each passing second.

A hatch flew open then, and Angar looked out from inside the ship. "Get in here!" He gestured for Tork to join him. "And *hurry!*" Then he disappeared down the hatchway.

Without hesitation, Tork ran over and scrambled down the ladder. No sooner had he slammed the hatch shut behind him than *Dark Dragon One* leaped away from the Gossa army.

Then swooped back with guns blazing to raze the shipyard, turning all the hundreds of spacecraft into blossoms of flame and fury.

EPILOGUE

HELLCYON

TORK'S HEART BEAT FAST AS HE STEPPED OUT OF *DARK Dragon One* onto the flight deck of the *Hellcyon*. For the first time in months, he smelled the ship's familiar atmosphere, heard the familiar echo of boots on the deck, and saw the familiar surroundings of the cavernous, gleaming chamber.

Until that moment, he hadn't realized just how good it would feel to be back.

"What a day!" Angar stomped out after him, swinging his sword. "I just want to eat, drink, and go right to bed!"

"Sounds good to me." Schist emerged next, his crystalline form glowing with the lavender light of gratitude. "That trip through the blockade really took it out of me."

Schist patted Tork on the shoulder on his way past, and Tork smiled. The flight from the surface had been a challenge, as the battle was still in progress. It had taken some incredible flying to dodge or blast all the enemy ships that had come after them in orbit.

In the end, though, *Dark Dragon One* had reached the *Hellcyon*, damaged yet intact. In response to Schist's hail, the ship had opened the doors on the flight deck, allowing the *Dragon* to come aboard.

At last, after the ordeal of Tork's life, things could get back to normal.

"I wouldn't mind some rest myself." Tork fell in step behind Angar and Schist. "You can get me caught up on everything tomorrow, huh?"

"Good plan." Angar laughed. "You missed out on a lot of *shang*."

Just then, the door to the corridor dissolved, and a detail of armed and armored security officers charged into the room. Before anyone could say a word, they lined up in front of the Horde Lords and Schist with weapons raised.

They were followed by Rerox Demagorn, who needed no armor beyond his naturally ironclad body. "Stop right there, you three!" he shouted. "Put down your weapons!"

"What the *shang?*" said Angar.

"I said *put them down!*" Rerox raised his energy rifle and pointed it at Angar. "That's a *direct order* from the *Captain!*"

"Like *shang* it is!" Angar took a step toward him.

"*It is!*" Another voice spoke from the doorway, a familiar voice…the singsong voice of a fallen goddess. "For *I* have given the order, my friends!"

Angar instantly lowered his sword, transfixed by the

sight of the woman who'd walked up beside Rerox. "Quinza?"

Butterflies fluttered on her head as she smiled grimly and nodded. "I promise you, the order came directly from me," said Quinza Acquiesce, "and I assure you, I *am* the captain of the *Hellcyon!*"

TO BE CONTINUED...

ABOUT THE AUTHOR

Robert Jeschonek is an envelope-pushing, *USA Today* best-selling author whose fiction, comics, and non-fiction have been published around the world. His stories have appeared in *Clarkesworld, Galaxy's Edge, StarShipSofa, Pulp-house,* and many other publications. He has written official *Star Trek* and *Doctor Who* fiction and has scripted comics for DC, AHOY, and others. His young adult slipstream novel, *My Favorite Band Does Not Exist,* won the Forward National Literature Award and was named one of *Book-list's* Top Ten First Novels for Youth. He also won an International Book Award, a Scribe Award for Best Original Novel, and the grand prize in Pocket Books' Strange New Worlds contest. Visit him online at www.bobscribe.-com. You can also find him on Facebook and follow him as @TheFictioneer on Twitter.

18 scifi stories from the edge of reality, now on sale for your favorite e-reading device or app.

From "The Stars So Black, The Space So White"

Imagine standing in the prow of a great sailing vessel, gazing out at the starry darkness as it folds around the nose of the ship. Now imagine the ship is in space.

And you are standing on an onyx gangplank, a sheer, black surface reflecting the starlight all around--creating the illusion that you are suspended without support in the void. Exposed to the nip and tug of so many rays and waves and streams and particles, yet somehow protected.

Watch as crackling suns and jewel-like worlds spin past. Wonder at the feathery, pastel tendrils of glowing nebulae. Grin with delight, because no matter how many times you see this, you can't help but marvel.

I can't help but marvel.

Welcome to my life. From Earthbound bartender savant to crewman on an alien spacecraft. From man of 20th century Earth to man of the cosmos.

You wish you were me. You *totally* wish you were me.

"I should have known." The voice behind me is high-pitched and piping with a fluttery vibrato. "I would find you here. Rudeee Tabernacle."

Turning, I smile at the dozens of multifaceted silver eyes staring my way, twisting on the ends of pale yellow tendrils. The tendrils are rooted in a glittering, creamy cloud, a misty blur of ever-shifting size and shape that hovers a meter above the onyx gangplank. Who knew I could come to love and respect someone so alien?

Who knew I could come to see my *abductor* as my *friend*?

"You are not feeling. Worried, are you?" The voice

emanates from somewhere in the cloud. It's the same voice I first heard fifty years ago, asking a question that changed my life forever and led me to this moment.

"Only hopeful." I bow, as is the custom in the fleet of the civilization whose name translates as The Rising. After fifty years among The Rising (though I look half as old as that, thanks to alien rejuvenation techniques), I know all the right things to do and say...though I don't always do and say them. But that, too, is customary; it's part of my job, after all.

They call me a *Chancer*. An X-factor in a social hierarchy with too much order...and a need for controlled chaos in the face of a highly improvisational universe.

As for the alien, if you called him/her/it/them a captain/teacher/lama/inexplicable presence, you wouldn't be wrong. "We approach. The source of. The signal."

His/her/its/their actual name is unpronounceable for a human like me, so I go with a boiled-down nickname. "Most Eager, has the content of the signal changed?"

Most Eager hiss-cough-squeals in a way that equates to a human head-shake. "The signal continues. To repeat."

I know the message by heart by now. "*Black stars. White space. Forever screaming.*"

"We will be there. Soon, Rudeee. The..." He calls our giant vessel by the name its builders gave it, which translates like this (more or less): *Peacefaring Manyfold Transitory Translightenment Construct, Constant.* "...will arrive within. The hour."

I shorten the ship's name like always. "The *Transit*'s ready, Most Eager. We'll do what we do best."

"Answer questions." Most Eager stiffens all

his/her/its/their tendrils at once like stalks in a cornfield. It's a salute. "Save lives."

I answer with a salute of my own, holding both fists at shoulder height, opening them into flattened palms. "And set the stage for tomorrow."

Setting the stage is The Rising's truest mission, our reason for being among the stars in the first place. The galaxy is full of lifeforms in varying degrees of evolution; we create mysteries that will draw them out here when the time is right to join the community of starfaring beings.

Speaking of mysteries, a ship like our own comes into view up ahead--a cluster of giant black shapeshifting objects, spherical at the moment like a bunch of grapes or a clutch of atoms in a molecule. The spheres, which normally blink with multicolored lights, are dark--and cut in half down the middle, wedged in a swirling halo of bright blue light.

"Do you think. They are still. Alive?" asks Most Eager.

I know he/she/it/they can tell if I'm lying, but I do it anyway. "Of course." After all, he/she/it/they has/have kin on that vessel.

More than kin. More like a protégé beloved above all others. And a *human*, like me.

Her name is Julie. And it is *her* voice--the voice of the trapped ship's first officer--repeating that message, over and over:

"Black stars. White space. Forever screaming."

∼

What happens next? Find out in <u>Blastoff!</u>, now available for your favorite e-reading device or app!